Sea Captain f

(continued from front ...)

Sea Captain
from
Salem

Ariel Books by Leonard Wibberley

Fiction

SEA CAPTAIN FROM SALEM

PETER TREEGATE'S WAR

JOHN TREEGATE'S MUSKET

KEVIN O'CONNOR AND THE LIGHT BRIGADE

THE WOUND OF PETER WAYNE

DEADMEN'S CAVE

THE SECRET OF THE HAWK

THE KING'S BEARD

Non-fiction

WES POWELL, CONQUEROR OF THE
GRAND CANYON

JOHN BARRY, FATHER OF THE NAVY

THE LIFE OF WINSTON CHURCHILL

THE EPICS OF EVEREST

THE CORONATION BOOK

Sea Captain
from
Salem

by
LEONARD
WIBBERLEY

Ariel Books
Farrar, Straus and Company · New York

Ariel Books is a division of Farrar, Straus and
Company, Inc. Published simultaneously in Canada
by Ambassador Books, Ltd., Toronto.

Manufactured in the United States of America
By H. Wolff

Sea Captain
from
Salem

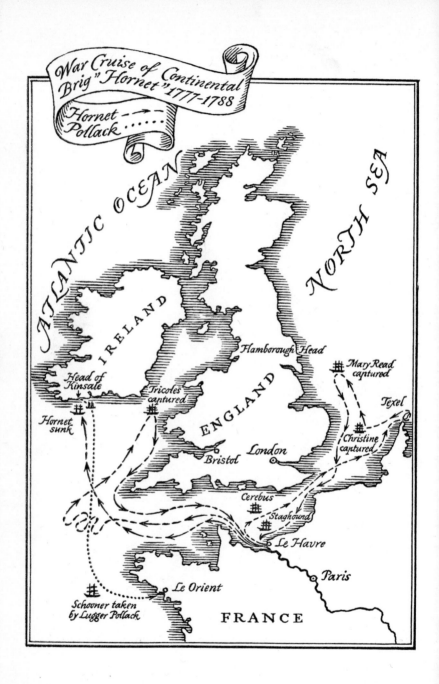

War Cruise of Continental
Brig "Hornet" 1777-1788

Hornet -----→
Pollack ....

ATLANTIC OCEAN

NORTH SEA

IRELAND

ENGLAND

Flamborough Head

Head of
Kinsale

Tricoles
captured

Hornet
sunk

Mary Read
captured

Texel

Christine
captured

Bristol

London

Cerebus

Staghound

Le Havre

Paris

Le Orient

Schooner taken
by Lugger Pollack

FRANCE

Continental Sloop of War

HORNET

Lugger

POLLACK

1

The sea fog, which had been rolling upon the Channel for a week now, had finally made its way to Paris and rolled slowly and with a touch of mystery over the innumerable roofs and chimney pots of that great city—the greatest and the fairest in all Europe.

It was white and thick, and filled the streets and muffled all the sounds—the clacking of the sabots of the workmen and the clatter of the wheels of drays and coaches over the cobblestones. Even the booming of the great bell of the church of St. Madeleine, striking the hour of ten at night, was muted by the sea mist as if bell and church were buried in the ground.

A man stood at a window in a house on the right bank of the Seine looking out at the fog. He was a short, solidly built man, but old almost to the point of being venerable. He wore a good plain suit, square cut with a touch of the Quaker to it. His breeches were gathered at the knee with a horn buckle where others might have worn silver, and his stockings were not silk but worsted. He did not wear a wig, though wigs were now in the height of fashion. His hair was long and white and came to his shoulders. But it was an old man's hair and came from a bald pate now covered, somewhat ridiculously, with a black square of cloth against the evil humors of the fog.

"Three weeks from America, eh, Captain?" said the man at the window, turning to another who sat gingerly on the edge of a chair, warming himself by a small fire.

"God gave me fair winds and a good passage, Dr. Franklin, sinner though I be," said the other, and he said this with great sincerity, as if it were a prayer or at least as if the Lord were in the room, listening to the words.

"Mind you," he added, "I kept me topsails flying and swung a mite north to get the best of the current. It don't do in fetching the Channel to fall too far south, for then there's the current, you see, that must be crossed and you must haul your wind and lose time and distance. But that be but seamanly and I don't speak with pride, for all skill comes from our Maker and nothing can be done without His giving you the nod."

Dr. Franklin nodded gravely. "And what might be your first name, Captain Manly?" he asked.

"Peace of God," replied the other. "I be one of John Wesley's flock of sinners."

"And your home town?"

"Salem, Massachussetts. I never thought to find myself in this heathen part. 'Tis like a Babylon, full of vice and wickedness and vain pride, so I have heard."

"And you would like to be back in Salem?"

"So I would, Dr. Franklin. So I would. To see my Nancy, that's seventeen this year and I haven't seen her since the start of the war—that being two years ago."

"And what would you say if I asked you to stay in these waters, on this side of the ocean?"

"Well, sir," said the other. "Duty is duty and that's all that there is to be said on that head."

For a moment Benjamin Franklin felt a twinge of regret at having to detain this seaman from Massachusetts in European waters and endanger his life. He was not a fighting kind of seaman, born to war, as it were, like John Paul Jones. He did not seek glory or death in battle. He came to war patiently, doggedly, determined to do his duty.

But he would sooner be back in Salem with his fishing boat, taking a few herring or cod, getting a lobster now and again out of his pots and going to church on Sundays, scrubbed and cleanly dressed and with his daughter Nancy on his arm. It was hard to take men such as this one and put their lives in jeopardy.

Benjamin Franklin knew the war record of the man who sat before him with a mixture of both doggedness and humility. Dr. Franklin knew that this man, Peace of God Manly, had been present at the battle of Breed's

(Bunker) Hill as a member of a company raised in Massachussetts and had been captured after that battle. He had been put on the prison hulks in Boston Harbor by the British and had contrived to escape because of his knowledge of the tidal flow around the prison hulks. He had been present at the battles of Trenton and Princeton and later at Saratoga . . . a sailor fighting ashore for a cause which he could only dimly perceive. Yet fighting because that was his duty both to his country and to God.

Dr. Franklin knew all these things because he made it his business to obtain a dossier on every man who was sent to him on a mission from the Colonies. But what he did not know, and was only now beginning to sense, was the man's deep attachment to his home in Salem and to his daughter Nancy. He assumed Peace of God was a widower. He was glad to find him a humble, religious and determined man, for he had need of such a man now. He had fought on land. But could he fight on sea? That was an important point.

"You are aware of the news you brought me?" Dr. Franklin asked.

"No," said Peace of God. "I were given a sealed packet by Mr. John Treegate in Boston—him that's in charge of the Continental Navy—and told to bring it to thee here in Paris."

"The packet contained the news of the surrender of General Burgoyne to the American forces at Saratoga," said Dr. Franklin. "It is tremendous news for us. The British will have their version and will try to make it look like a victory for them or at least a small loss of no consequence. But we have the news first, and the story of Burgoyne's surrender will have a great influence on the French. Nothing could be better for us at this time."

"I don't see that it is any of their affair," said Peace of God.

"Well," said Dr. Franklin with a smile, "maybe it isn't but I intend that it shall be." He glanced at the fire in the grate. It was a modest fire and did little to heat the large room the two were in. Dr. Franklin hesitated a moment and then picked up a piece of coal with a pair of tongs and put it on the fire. He fiddled with the coal for a while, positioning it on the fire, and watched as a stream of smoke arose from it; yellowish smoke that slipped up the chimney and then in a moment caught fire.

"There is an inflammable gas in that coal," said Dr. Franklin, "and if some means might be contrived of extracting it, I have no doubt that it would serve both to illuminate and heat houses. It might also be used to cook with."

He seemed to have utterly forgotten for a moment the news of the surrender of Burgoyne, the impact this would have upon the French court, the sea captain who still sat gingerly on the chair before him, and indeed, the whole war between the American Colonies and the mother country.

Indeed, he got up from before the fire and went to a writing desk and taking a piece of paper scribbled something upon it with a quill which squeaked while he wrote. Then he looked over what he had written, folded the paper and put it in the flap pocket of his frock coat.

"If it were heated in some kind of a closed container, so that no flame got to it, the gas might be driven off in that manner and collected in a suitable receptacle for use."

"So it might, sir," said Peace of God Manly, "but we were talking of the French."

"Ah yes," said Dr. Franklin with regret. "Well, the French have been enemies of the British for many hundreds of years. They still feel very keenly their defeat in the French and Indian wars which cost them Canada. They are disposed to help us, as a result of this ancient enmity, but are hesitating.

"They have reasons for hesitating. Though they lost an empire in America and another in India, they still have colonies in the West Indies. If they were drawn into a war on our behalf with Britain—and lost again— they might lose their possessions in the West Indies. This is one reason why they hesitate. Yet we must draw them in on our side.

"This surrender of Burgoyne's, properly used, may well do the trick. The French will think now of winning and not losing the war with Britain. We don't need their manpower. But we need their navy to cut off the British supplies to their army in America. And we need arms from them. Given these two aids, victory is but a matter of time.

"And for these reasons, I have to keep you in European waters for a while and not let you go back to Salem and your Nancy."

"I'll do what is asked of me," said Peace of God slowly, "that being my duty. But I do not understand what is in thy mind."

"Tell me, Captain Manly," said Dr. Franklin, "have you ever fought a sea battle? Have you ever been in any kind of sea engagement?"

"I took the brig *Betsy* into Lynn when she was being chased by a British frigate," said the other. " 'Twere a matter of navigating—taking an inland passage with a tide race ahead—but I had God's wind behind me and drew but a fathom, and so came safely home." *

"Ah . . . And your ship now is a brig?"

"It is. Maine built. The *Hornet.*"

"A fast sailer?"

"She is that," said Peace of God. "She will lie as close to the wind as a weather cock but running she is as foolish as a sheep and will jibe all standing unless there is a good man at the helm. 'Tis her foremast does it. 'Tis stepped too far forward and brings her head down. The Maine boats are all built so, being used more for working to windward than running before. But she does well on a quartering wind, though she fights her helm."

It was plain that Peace of God assumed that the significance of sea talk was perfectly clear to Dr. Franklin. He had spent all his life at sea and indeed knew of no other kind of life. What was perfectly clear

* See *Peter Treegate's War.*

and simple to him then, he was certain must be clear to everybody else, for he could not conceive that there were men who did not know such necessary matters as how to sail a boat or the characteristics of different vessels in different winds.

"What armament do you carry?" asked Franklin.

"Eight eight-pounders—four to a broadside. Four four-pounders on the poop, and a bow chaser of eight pounds up forward."

"Excellent," said Dr. Franklin. "And you have powder and shot?"

Peace of God shook his head. "I have four tubs of powder and enough shot for three broadsides and no more. That was all that could be spared when I cleared Boston."

"Well," said Dr. Franklin, "that is something I can provide. I will give you a note to the Marquis of Echemont in Le Havre and he will supply what you need.

"Now to what I have in mind.

"I have already spoken of the agelong enmity between France and England and of our desire to enlist French aid. One way of doing this is obvious—to impress the French with the victories we have achieved in the Colonies. If they think we are going to win, they will join us.

"Another method is not so obvious. It is to increase the enmity between Britain and France—to do all we can to get these two nations at each other's throats. In short, to bring them to the point of war one with the other.

"It is here that I need your services.

"In brief, when your brig the *Hornet* is fully equipped, I want you to sail on a war cruise in the English Channel and around the British Isles. You are to attack any British vessels you may come upon— fishing smacks, coastal brigs, sloops of war—anything you can find and have a fair prospect of taking as a prize or sinking.

"All the prizes you take you are to bring into French harbors—Le Havre or L'Orient on the Atlantic coast if possible—where they will be sold and you will receive your share of the sale. The British are becoming increasingly angered at the French for selling us arms. They will be all the more angered if American privateers operate out of French ports sinking and capturing British vessels. That is all to our purpose. Have you any questions, Captain?"

"Did you say fishing smacks?" asked Peace of God.

"I did," replied Dr. Franklin.

"Fishing be a hard life for a man," said Peace of God. "There's some that's called to it, that being their service on earth as God intended, and so must do the work. I don't complain about it, having been a fisherman myself these forty years, but 'tis a hard life nonetheless. There's the labor at the nets, do you see, with your hands so cold your bones feel like they're turned to iron.

"Then there's storms and the cold of winter and the roaring of the sea and lobster pots lost and gear that carries away and must be replaced. I'd feel badly to come upon a fisherman with my cannon and take his boat that he may not have paid for, and his nets that he's spent many hours mending, and his fish and gear, and bring him over to France and sell them all, and him left a prisoner in a foreign land. Even if he were an Englishman. For fishermen, do you see, are fishermen, and help each other, their life being cruel hard. And so I'd feel mortal bad to take any fishing smacks to make the King of England wrathful against the King of France—and neither of them ever met a fisherman in their lives."

At the end of this talk, delivered with great solemnity, Dr. Franklin was chuckling with mirth. He took off his wire-rimmed spectacles to wipe his eyes and then fished a large plain handkerchief out of his side pocket and in an effort to regain his dignity, blew his nose with unnecessary force.

"I had never thought," he said, still chuckling, "that high affairs of state might be brought to nothing by this freemasonry among fishermen. But never mind. I absolve you from attacking fishing smacks. All I ask of you is that you do not stop and help them to haul in their nets while on this war cruise. Can I rely on you there?"

"To that I will agree," said Peace of God gravely.

"Good. Now I will give you a note to the Marquis of Echemont for whatever supplies you may need. You will find him at the premises of Echemont et Cie, rue des Pecheurs in Le Havre." Seeing the puzzled look on Peace of God's face, he added, "I will write it down for you. You can draw on him for all the supplies you need, and I will settle the account.

"On one matter I want to caution you. Your vessel is now in Le Havre and you can be sure that news that it is there has already been sent by British agents to the British naval forces in the Channel. When you try to clear Le Havre, you will probably find a frigate waiting for you outside the three-mile limit. She will probably be the *Cerebus* of thirty-two guns. That is her usual station. Her captain is Sir Thomas Greenhow—an excellent man. How you are to elude the frigate is your business. But I suggest you sail at night and make use of the Channel fog to get away. But let nobody know—not even your crew—when you are to sail. Le Havre is thick with British spies.

"And about your daughter Nancy. If you wish to write her a letter, I will see that it reaches her by the first ship to leave." He paused a moment, and then said, "If you cannot write, dictate what you wish to say and I will set it down for you."

"I can print well, though slow," said Peace of God.

Dr. Franklin waved the seaman to the writing table. Peace of God crossed to the table and stood before it for a moment, clenching and unclenching his fists as if to get the muscles of his hand in good condition for a difficult job that lay before them.

Then he sat down and, taking a quill from among several on the desk, licked it and tried it on the paper, moving it up and down to see how the point served. This done he stood and took off his sea coat and folded it and put it neatly on the floor and seated himself again.

Then he dipped the quill in the ink and started his letter. He worked as under a great strain, his tongue protruding from the corner of his mouth with the effort, and his face moving as he formed the letters.

"*My dear daughter,*" he wrote, printing each letter, *for he had no skill with script.* "*I be in France upon my duty and do not know when I will be home to see thee, that all lying as God may decide to Whose will we must all be obedient. I have good health and eat hearty but not above what is needed and hope you do likewise.*

"*The boat will need another coat of pitch. See that it is laid on hot along the garboard strakes and not too thick. There is a bad plank near the starboard chine but do not fret about it. It will hold for another year. The net in the loft will go moldy if air is not let to it. Do thou get it down and spread it on the wall in the south field and let it air two days and put it back in the loft. See that it is dry before you put it back, for damp will rot it and it cost twenty-five shillings and that but two years ago.*

"*I will bring back some present from France for you, but do not set your heart on lace. Lace is Satan's favorite snare, being a sign of vanity by which the angels fell. But perhaps a ribbon for your hair would suit if it is worn for use and not vain ornament. I think you spoke of a blue ribbon once and I will find one for you.*

"*Mr. Peter Treegate of Boston may call upon you, for I asked him to inquire into your health and needs before leaving. He was brought up in the wilds among savages and Scotsmen, but God spared him and brought him to Boston. He will offer you what help he can, but see he is out of the house by sundown and let your talk be modest and dwell frequently upon Christian doctrine.*

"There is a fog upon the ocean and the wind is but a whisper and from the west.

Your loving father,
Peace of God."

The writing of this letter took the better part of half an hour. When it was done, Peace of God folded it and handed it to Dr. Franklin and returned to the chair by the fire.

Dr. Franklin then sat at the writing table to compose his letter to the Marquis of Echemont at Le Havre.

Outside the fog had thickened so that the city and indeed all the world seemed to have disappeared, leaving as sole survivors these two strangely associated men in the candlelit room.

2

⚓

The premises of Echemont et Cie on the rue des Pecheurs in Le Havre proved to be a number of ancient barnlike buildings tottering against each other so that it seemed that one good blow, or a gust of wind, would send them all reeling to the ground. The buildings were of wood, and the wood came from ships of various kinds that had been dismantled. There was therefore no attempt at design in erecting the four or five buildings which together comprised the facilities of the company. They had been rough carpentered together with odds and ends of lumber, and the very boat nails that came from the wrecks had been used again for fastenings.

Peace of God felt that the buildings were matched to the people of France. He had never seen people in such wretched conditions. He was a poor man himself, in terms of money, and ten pounds a year was all that passed through his hands. But his clothes were neatly darned and well made of good materials.

His sea boots were of excellent leather, hand-sewn by a cobbler at Lynn, and the stocking cap which he wore upon his head, knitted by his daughter Nancy, was of good three-ply wool and would last many a year. In contrast, there did not seem to be among the common people of France one who had ever had a new suit of clothes in his life. All were in rags; their *pantalons,* as they called them, reaching hardly below the knee and the bottoms torn, and their shirts made in some cases of flour sacks and nothing seemingly ever darned or washed.

They wore no stockings, neither men nor women, and their naked feet were thrust into shoes of wood which they called sabots and which clacked over the filthy cobbles of the streets producing a continuing hubbub. The streets of Paris were in passable shape, but the streets of Le Havre were vile. In many places the cobbles had been dug up for building material by the wretched inhabitants, and the resulting holes were filled with foul water where little children, raucous, dirty and thin as sticks, sailed toy boats contrived of a piece of wood or sometimes a wooden shoe. They did this in peril of their lives, for through the streets and over these potholes carters drove their drays at a furious rate, cracking their whips and urging their teams on without regard for the danger to the children.

Near the wharves, where Echemont and Cie had their premises, the cart traffic was especially heavy, drays, wagons, carriages, coaches, sedan chairs and hand barrows all mixed up together in a terrible tangle, with all the drivers of the drays screaming at the drivers of the coaches, and the outriders of the coaches trying to clear a way with their whips, and the people with the hand barrows cursing the coaches and the drays and the wagons and the coachmen and the outriders. Indeed, it seemed that at any moment some terrible violence would occur, a riot in which several would be slain and others trampled under the hoofs of the horses or crushed beneath the heavy wheels. But nothing of the sort happened. This seemed to be just the normal conduct of the traffic in the streets of Le Havre.

Through all this hubbub and after being misdirected many times, Peace of God made his way to the warehouses of Echemont et Cie—a solid, quiet, patient figure in the midst of chaos. He had come by water from Paris and disembarked at a jetty, and there had been an argument with the boatman who had, by signs, demanded more money than was agreed for the passage. Peace of God, by signs, resisted this demand. The boatman grew furious. Peace of God remained quiet. The boatman appealed to several people at the jetty, denouncing this foreigner who was trying to cheat an honest French waterman of his wage, and the crowd, lacking other sport, had thought it would be fun to assist the boatman in throwing Peace of God into the filthy river, on the ground that he was a foreigner and, furthermore, an Englishman.

Two boarded the boat to assist in this project, whereupon Peace of God solemnly picked up the heavy wooden bailing bucket. This produced a setback, the three men at one end of the boat eying the small resolute figure with the heavy bailing bucket at the other.

Peace of God seized this interruption to address the three Frenchmen. He spoke in English, for he assumed, since English was his own tongue, that all the world spoke English, as he assumed that all men knew something of handling boats. All that was required was to speak slowly and these Frenchmen would understand him.

"Fellow sinners," he said, "let us not add to our offenses in the sight of God which are numerous on my part and, I have no doubt, are on yours also (for you live in a sinful and unpious land) by fighting with each other. But let us behave toward each other as the little lambs in the meadows who are without guile and a lesson to all men. However, if your hearts are inclined to evil as they seem to be, reflect that I will, though with sorrow, with this bucket stave in the head of the first man who lays hands on me."

The three Frenchmen eyed the seaman from Salem with a lessening of zeal, and the boatman, hoping to encourage his allies said, "English pig" and spat at Peace of God. The words were in English, and Peace of God replied:

"I am not English but American. And though in the eyes of our Creator all men are brothers, yet there is some difference here upon earth."

The Frenchmen caught only the word American and now their attitude completely changed. They were all smiles. Demands for more money were dropped, and Peace of God was assisted out of the boat as if he were a lifelong friend and patron of the very boatman who had been on the point of throwing him into the river but a moment previously. Indeed, the boatman, having made an impromptu address, quite incomprehensible to Peace of God, about the Americans to the others on the wharf, demanded that they immediately clear a passage and let him go on his business.

One man, not moving aside smartly enough to suit the boatman, was given a kick by the latter to stir him to greater courtesy. And so Peace of God went his way, wondering at the ways of the French, and came at last to the warehouse he sought.

He entered through a door which he recognized had once belonged to the great cabin of a ship and found himself facing a long counter at which a thin clerk, the sleeves of whose jacket came only a third of the way down his bony arms, was making an entry in a ledger. A man was sitting on the counter at the one end. His feet were stretched along the surface of the counter and his back propped against the wall. He was engaged in cutting a piece of paper with a pair of scissors and so intent on this task that he did not even look up when Peace of God entered.

Peace of God had a great respect for anyone who

could write and never interrupted those engaged in this difficult task, so he stood for a little time while the clerk finished what he was doing. The clerk was in no hurry. Having but a lowly position in life, it was necessary for him to make every possible use of such authority delegated to him and make it appear that he was a man of some importance.

One method of doing this was to occupy himself with his ledger whenever anyone required waiting upon. Indeed, it was his habit, as soon as the door of the warehouse opened, to reach for his quill pen, don his spectacles and open up the ledger as if to make some entry, though in truth he often had no entry to make. The clerk therefore continued with his writing in the ledger and when it was done, without a glance at Peace of God, opened the book in another place, inspected a row of figures there, pursed his lips, took off his glasses, shook his head, replaced his glasses and continued poring over the page. Meanwhile the other individual at the end of the counter continued cutting the design out of the piece of paper, and Peace of God stood humbly aside, waiting to be noticed.

Eventually the clerk pushed the ledger aside and looked up, saw Peace of God as if for the first time, clucked with irritation and asked in French what might be his business.

"I would like to see the Marquis of Echemont," replied the seaman.

"He would like to see the marquis," repeated the clerk to the man who was cutting the paper at the end of the counter. He spoke in English.

"Very interesting," said the other, continuing with his cutting. "He'll be an American," he added. "Wants powder and shot most likely. And maybe the name of a tavern where the brandy is cheap."

"I would have nothing to do with such sinful thoughts," said Peace of God, "and you should be ashamed to utter them."

"In that case," said the man with the scissors, still working upon the paper, "he'll be from New England."

"What is your name?" asked the clerk.

"Peace of God Manly," said the other. "I be one of John Wesley's flock."

At this the man with the scissors looked up from his work for the first time and gave Peace of God a thorough scrutiny as if he were a rare type of human being whom he was not likely to meet again.

"You have a letter for the marquis?" asked the clerk.

"I have," said Peace of God.

"If you will leave it with me and return tomorrow," said the clerk, "I will see that he gets it and you shall have your answer."

Peace of God thought about this for a few seconds. He produced the letter and, turning it over in his hands, examined it for a little while.

" 'Tis written in English," he said.

"So?" said the clerk surprised.

"It isn't more than perhaps two score words," continued the other.

"So?" repeated the clerk.

"So I don't think it would take the marquis all the time from today until tomorrow to read it," said Peace of God, quite gravely. "Should be no difficult task, though 'tis in script and that's hard to figure the way the letters run into each other. But if a man were to put his mind to it, I'd say that half an hour would be enough to read it through and get the sense of it and give an answer and get under way again on whatever were his course before."

At this there was a stifled explosion of laughter from the gentleman, still sitting upon the end of the counter, who was busy cutting up the paper, and the clerk looked at him angrily and then snapped shut the big ledger before him so that it made a muffled report, and snatched the letter from Peace of God. He looked it over as if by examination of the envelope to ascertain the contents and then, without another word and still flushed with anger, walked into the back of the storehouse, among the shelves and bins and bales until he was lost to sight, though his footsteps could be heard ascending a flight of stairs somewhere to the rear.

Peace of God heaved a sigh of relief and, turning gently to the man with the scissors, said, "Brother, I mean no offense and yet I think you are in great danger."

The other stiffened almost imperceptibly. His scissors stopped for a second in their clipping and then he went on with his work and without looking up said, "Danger? All men are in danger from the moment of their birth to the time of their death. Life would be . . . ah . . . tedious without it."

His voice was certainly an English voice, Peace of God reflected. The inflection and tone and choice of words were those of the English officers he had heard talking during the time he had been a prisoner on a hulk in Boston Harbor early in the war.

"I wasn't talking of any ordinary danger, brother," said Peace of God, "but of a peril so great, so powerful and so overwhelming that the very thought of it makes me sweat with fear for you."

"Most interesting," said the man with the scissors. "And pray what peril might that be?"

"Idleness," said Peace of God gravely. "Idleness. For the devil finds work for idle hands and idle minds. And idleness is the great highway down which men go carelessly into the pit of hell, there to burn in the sulphurous fires in torments and wailings for all eternity."

At this the man put down his scissors and looked at Peace of God in sheer amazement. Then he put back his head and laughed, a great horse's neigh of a laugh, and he added to the effect by kicking his feet with delight upon the counter top while Peace of God looked at him solemnly, shaking his head from side to side in warning at such levity.

" 'The loud laugh,' " he said when the other had done, " 'that bespeaks the vacant mind.' "

"I hadn't thought to hear a New England fisherman quoting Goldsmith," said the other. "Are you familiar with Gray also?"

"No," said Peace of God. "The Bible, *The Deserted Village* and *Appeals to Men of Reason and Religion* by the Reverend John Wesley. These are the mainstays of my life. I earnestly urge you to read and ponder on them all, for in them you will find the seeds of salvation from sin and escape from the wrath to come."

"I will promise nothing," said the other, "and yet you are wrong to accuse me of idleness. What looks like idleness to one is work to another."

At this juncture the clerk returned and without a word opened a flap in the counter top and beckoned Peace of God to follow him. He was led to the back of the huge warehouse, past coils of ropes and barrels of chains and others of shot and others of flour and pork and bolts of canvas and all the stock of a ship chandlery, to a flight of stairs. The two went up these stairs arriving at a rickety landing also made of scrap lumber, at one end of which was a door. The clerk knocked on the door, waited for a second, and then opening it, beckoned Peace of God to follow him.

He went down three ancient steps to find himself in a small room, not much larger than the cabin of a frigate, and hopelessly cluttered with stacks of cloth and stacks of paper, bins, barrels and packing cases, oblong in shape, some opened and filled seemingly with straw and others nailed shut. The room was so dark that a cluster of lanterns hanging from a beam in the ceiling was needed to give illumination. Peace of God noted that there was no window in the room, though overhead there was a trap door in the ceiling, or rather in the roof, which contained a dirty and cracked pane of glass.

In this morass of goods there was a small table and, seated at the table, a man plainly dressed in brown worsted who was waiting for him. The man had a long thin chin and a long thin nose, the two of them making, as it were, the lower and upper parts of a beak. His face, in the dim light, seemed chalk white, but his eyes were dark and lively with humor.

"Sit down," said this individual, motioning to a barrel near his table and he nodded a dismissal to the clerk who withdrew.

"Now," said the man briskly, when they were alone, "your credentials."

"Credentials?"

"Your papers of identity?"

"Why to be sure," said the seaman. He reached into an inner pocket of his coat, took out an oilskin packet tied together with tarred string, undid this and extracted a certificate which he gave to the other. It attested that Peace of God Manly, by order of the Marine Committee and with the assent of the Congress of the United States, had been commissioned a captain in the Continental Navy and assigned to the command of the sloop of war *Hornet*. The signature was that of John Treegate, chairman of the Marine Committee at Boston.

"This letter from Dr. Franklin asks me to supply you with powder and shot and whatever else you may need," said the other. "What are your requirements?"

"Of shot ten barrels for eight-pounders," said Peace of God, "and four barrels for four-pounders. And of powder, two ton. Also four hogsheads of salt beef and four of ship's biscuit."

"Anything else?" asked the other.

"A chart of the waters around the British Isles," said Peace of God. "And half a dozen French flags."

At this the man behind the table pursed his lips in a meditative manner, opened the lid of the inkwell before him and shut it again, and fumbled for a few moments with the sandbox and quills which were also on the table.

"High stakes," he said at length. "High stakes." And then he shrugged and added, "But I have always preferred to wager for high stakes. Your stores will be aboard by noon tomorrow. The receipt for them which you will sign will show merely that you have been provisioned with ship's biscuit, salt pork, rope, canvas and other stores. The barrels of powder will be marked with a blue cross on the head of the barrel. Your charts will be given you by one of the carters. You are aware that the frigate *Cerebus* lies off the mouth of the Seine on patrol?"

"Yes," said Peace of God.

"The fog should hold until tomorrow night," said the other. "And high tide is at nine in the evening."

"Is the *Cerebus* at anchor or standing on an off?" asked Peace of God.

"At anchor," replied the other. "You will find her position, as last known, marked on the charts I will give you."

"Why did you talk of high stakes, brother?" asked Peace of God.

"A sloop of war against an English frigate?" replied the other, and gave a sharp laugh not without mirth. "I would say those stakes were high enough. And this is no bumbling English squire of a sea captain aboard the frigate. There is a man in command who seems to have been born to fight at sea—Sir Thomas Greenhow. That makes the stakes higher. I do not think you have much chance, my friend, though I wish you luck."

"Luck is a pagan superstition," said Peace of God gravely. "I will do what I can and the issue will be with God, who ever has us in His care."

The other stared at him for a moment, surprised by this show of piety.

"You saw a man downstairs cutting paper with a scissors?"

"I did," said Peace of God. "His hands being idle, the devil's found work for them."

"He was not so idle," replied the marquis. "He is a spy in the English service. You wonder I allow him on the premises. But it is better, my friend, to know where a spy is than not to know where he is. Rest assured he will have you under constant watch and will communicate with the frigate *Cerebus* when you leave."

"The tide will be flowing full at. six in the evening," said Peace of God.

"It will," said the marquis.

"I will leave then," said Peace of God. "It would serve me if this man with the scissors heard of that."

The marquis shrugged. "As you wish," he said. He extended his hand. "Good luck to you," he said.

"It will not be luck," repeated Peace of God, "but God's will—to which I can only add such seamanship as He has seen fit, in His infinite goodness, to give me."

With that they parted.

3

At six in the evening of the following day the Continental sloop of war *Hornet* was creeping through the sea fog from the port of Le Havre into the Channel waters. Her course was west northwest by one half west and she carried full canvas to catch whatever breath of air might stir and help her on her way. But there was very little wind, and that dying. Her topsails and royals occasionally filled slowly and then collapsed as if filling had not been worth the effort. The crews of the two boats ahead of the *Hornet*, who were towing her against the tide for lack of wind, heartily cursed their work and grumbled that they could row for an hour and make half a mile.

Peace of God Manly stood by the helmsman near the break of the little poop deck, watching the compass needle as it swung left and right with the rolling of the ship but always centered on north. He was worried about the compass. It was out of true because of the amount of metal shot he had on board, and he had tried to correct for this deviation but was not sure of his calculations. The men on the boats were steering by compass also. Their compasses would not agree with the one on the *Hornet,* for they would not be affected by any metal around. The compasses on the boats would show a true north, the one on the *Hornet* a false north. By checking then what should be his course against the course the compass showed, Peace of God could find the error in the ship's compass. It was one of the things that seamen did—one of the hundreds of little calculations necessary for the safe navigation of ships at sea.

"The compass has an error of five degrees eastern deviation," said Peace of God. "See that your relief knows this when he takes over."

"Aye, aye, sir," said the helmsman. "Five degrees, eastern deviation." Then he added, "The tide's making faster."

"Yes," said Peace of God. "She's making faster and the further out we get the more we'll feel it."

"I heard the word passed that there's a frigate standing somewhere out there," said the helmsman, nodding to starboard.

"There is," said Peace of God. "Thirty-two guns."

"She'll have picket boats out, likely. The fog being so thick."

"That would be reasonable to expect," said Peace of God. He hoped that word of the time of his leaving had been sent to the captain of the frigate by the man with the scissors. It was part of his plan.

He moved away from the helmsman now, for the time had come for a final inspection of his ship before putting into action the plan he had worked out.

It was a daring plan, and he had consulted nobody about it, not even his first lieutenant Esek Hawkins who was out now on one of the boats ahead and was a man who was very sparse with words. He never said anything that was not absolutely necessary. Peace of God might have consulted Hawkins about his plan, confident that not a word of it would be passed to the crew. But he decided against it. To consult him would be merely to have him share in the blame if the plan went awry. If it went awry, it would mean the loss of the *Hornet* by gunfire and the death or capture of all the men aboard her.

Originally Peace of God had intended merely to pass to the westward of the frigate *Cerebus* in the fog, and thus gain the open Channel. From a purely navigational point of view it would have been easier to pass to the east. In that direction the inflowing tide which he was fighting against now would help him.

But this, he hoped, was what Captain Greenhow, the commander of the frigate *Cerebus*, would expect. And so the Englishman would have his picket boats to the east of his vessel, ready to board any ship passing in that direction. So Peace of God had chosen the westward route—the hard one, towing his ship against the tide and gambling that there would be no picket boats to spot him on that side.

He had laid his course to pass two miles to the west of the *Cerebus* on her unguarded side. Then another idea had occurred to him. He would be abreast of the *Cerebus* but two miles west of her at eight o'clock. At that time the tide would be flowing at five knots. In something less than half an hour, then, if he let the tide take the *Hornet,* she would come down on the *Cerebus.*

Why not come down upon her? Why not let the tide sweep him down on the anchored frigate and give her a broadside as he went past at five knots? She would be taken completely by surprise. The *Hornet* would be swept away in the mist in a matter of seconds, and the *Cerebus* would be unable to reply. Wouldn't that be what his duty called for—to attack whatever he could? A sloop of war, mounting only eight-pounders, was no match for a frigate in clear weather. The frigate's thirty-two-pounders could blow her out of the water with one broadside at a distance of two or three miles. But in a thick fog and with the frigate at anchor and unprepared, the odds were more even.

That, then, was his plan—to get two miles uptide of the frigate and then sweep down on her with the tide and give her a broadside as he went past. With luck he might hole her, or damage her rigging, or cut her cables, or bring down a few of her yards. It was useless, of course, to think of bringing down a mast. She could take a sixteen-pound shot in her masts without losing them. But she would feel the sting of the *Hornet,* and the story would soon be back in France that a little Continental sloop of war had attacked a British frigate. It would strengthen the American cause in the court of the French king and that was one of the things Dr. Franklin was intent upon.

So that was his plan. And now it was time to inspect the *Hornet* and see that the orders he had given, with the plan in view, had been put into effect.

He went first to the eight-pounder gun batteries and assured himself that the shot racks were full. The tubs containing the slow matches were in place beside each gun, the tops covered with canvas to prevent the damp getting at the fuses. The touchholes of the little guns were also wrapped with canvas, and there was a plug of hemp down the muzzles, again to prevent the wet air getting inside and causing a misfire. He checked that there was a gunner's spike by each piece. The spike would be inserted in the touchhole to puncture the paper cartridge when it had been inserted down the muzzle and let the fire of the slow match get at the powder. He'd drilled his men in this coming across the Atlantic, and they were accustomed to the routine. All was well with the guns, then, and he went below by the forward hatch to the powder room.

The powder room was in the very bowels of the brig. It was padded throughout with heavy felt. That was one of the things he had insisted upon before sailing. It had to be lit, for being deep down in the ship, the powder room was as black as the bottom of a well.

The illumination came from a lantern set in the walls of the powder room with a plate of thick glass before it. The lantern could not be taken out into the powder room but was reached by a well from the deck above. In the room, the master gunner, a red-faced, red-haired man named Simmons, was directing two powder boys who were making up paper cartridges on a small felt-covered table.

"French powder," he was saying, "ain't of the best. The frogs is a cheating people. The king cheats the nobles, and the nobles cheats the gentry, and the gentry cheats the farmers, and the farmers cheat the peasants, and that's the way it is with the French. And that being the case they cheats on everything they sell including their gunpowder, and their gunpowder ain't no good. At least, it ain't much good."

"Can you tell good gunpowder by looking at it?" asked one of the powder boys, named Dickie.

"Not by looking at it, you can't. But by biting on it. Now, you just take a little of that there powder and put it in the back of your mouth between your teeth and chomp down on it hard."

"What'll happen?" asked Dickie.

"Why, if it were good powder, which this ain't, it would explode and knock out your teeth. That's how come I lost all of mine. Chomping on powder for General Braddock in the Indian wars. You can always tell a master gunner because he ain't got no teeth. Ain't got no teeth but has a powerful thirst on account of the saltpeter in the powder. And that being the case, Dickie me lad, do you run aft and bring me the can of—

Well, hello, Captain. You come in so quiet I didn't hear you and 'tis so dark in here I didn't see you neither."

"Strong drink," said Peace of God, "is a device of Satan's to snare the unwary and make them his vassals for all eternity."

"Listen to what your captain says," said the master gunner, "for he never spoke a truer word."

"It is to you I am speaking, Mr. Simmons," said Peace of God. "You are weak and have not learned to wrestle with Satan. Yet if you do not fight with him tooth and nail, hip and thigh, he will overthrow you and drag you into the loathsome pit there to suffer and mourn forever more."

"Amen to that, sir, says I," replied the master gunner very cheerfully. "And yet do you think, sir, since we are discussing these spiritual matters, that Satan is here with us in this powder hold?"

"I do indeed," said Peace of God.

"Then he's a bolder spirit than I'd give him credit for, for if I had me druthers I'd be anywhere else but here where as little a thing as a spark could blow him and me to kingdom come. And in action 'tis something terrible as you must know yourself, sir, with the whole ship shaking, and the barrels of powder jostling each other, and the lantern jumping in its cupboard there, and the sounds of the guns round about as if they were firing in this very hold. Not a 'ealthy place for man nor devil at a time such as that, and while a man must stay here, why the devil, I expect, is free to take his self off until things quiet down a bit."

"I will have you on your knees praying God for forgiveness for your simple foolishnesses before this cruise is over," said Peace of God, very gently. "On your knees, crying for salvation. How many cartridges have you ready?"

"Fourscore, sir," replied the gunner.

"You are using double the amount of powder?"

"Aye, aye, sir. Double and a noggin more, this being French powder and not of the best."

"Keep the cartridges below, then, until I pass the word to bring them up," said Peace of God. "The powder is dry?"

"Dry as I am, sir," said Simmons, and the powder boys, watching the captain's face out of the corners of their eyes, caught a touch of a smile on it.

"This Captain Manly," said Dickie when Peace of God had gone, "sounds more like a parson than a sea captain."

"Well," said the master gunner, "a parson is a kind of a captain, steering you safe through bad water."

"Is he a fighting man?" asked the other powder boy.

"He is that," said the master gunner, "and there's something awful about him when he's in action. There's some that goes into a fight all hot and swearing and crying for blood. And there's others that goes in quiet but determined, keeping the anger in them back and their heads cool. But this here Peace of God Manly, he's got them all beat. He goes into a fight solemn and slow and deliberate, asking forgiveness for himself, and once he's started there ain't nothing but death will stop him until he's finished. Kind of chills you to think of it.

It ain't natural. Praying for his enemies and blowing them to kingdom come at the same time."

"Praying?" said the first powder boy.

"Aye. Praying," repeated the master gunner. "I seen him in the fight outside of Boston, on that hill, bring down a grenadier with a hanger and then go down on his knees beside him and pray for him. And right in the middle of it up comes another, and Peace of God left off praying just long enough to bring him down too. And then he kneels between the two of them, with the battle smoke drifting over them, and calls them poor sinners like himself and asks God to receive them joyfully into everlasting glory, amen."

"Seems odd to kill a man and then pray for him," said the powder boy named Dickie.

"Odd it is," replied the master gunner. "And yet if you take another look at it, it's odder yet to kill a man and not pray for him."

Peace of God had meanwhile gone to his cabin which was aft of the wheel under the poop deck. It had room for a bunk on one side and a table on the other and nothing else. His clothing hung from the deck beams overhead along the bulkheads, and though there were windows around the cabin, they were heavily curtained to prevent the light of a solitary lantern being seen outside. He sat at the table on which was spread a chart of the waters in which he was now sailing. On the chart, marked with a neat red cross, was the position of the frigate *Cerebus*. A faintly inked-in line on the chart gave the course of the *Hornet*. He fished a leather pouch out of the pocket of his coat and out of this took a heavy watch and, glancing at it, saw that it was now seven-thirty. With a pair of dividers he marked off the estimated position of the *Hornet* and, going to the door of his cabin, addressed the helmsman who stood immediately outside at the wheel with his back to him.

"Pass the word to take a sample of the bottom," he said. "No noise." Then he closed the cabin door and waited. A few minutes later and the bosun reported the sample, obtained by dropping a lead weight with some tallow on the end of it over the side of the ship.

"Sand and white shell at six fathoms," he said.

Peace of God turned to his chart. The bottom close to the shore was stated to be mud. A mile out it was sand. Two miles it was white shell and pebbles. Three miles out it was sand and white shell. He was over this area now and if his calculations were right two miles to the west of the frigate.

It was time to recall the boat crew from their labors, then, turn the *Hornet* around and drift down on the frigate.

Peace of God went out on deck to give the order.

4

Even with the nicest calculation, the chances of the *Hornet* finding the *Cerebus* in the fog—of drifting down upon her with the incoming tide—were slim. Visibility was less than a hundred feet. Beyond that nothing could be seen through the impenetrable silent white shroud of fog that hung over the Channel. So it was quite possible that the brig would glide past the frigate and neither would see each other.

Peace of God was well aware of this; aware that all depended upon his calculations and upon the accuracy of the chart on which the calculations were based.

His plan was simple. If the chart were accurate and gave a correct statement of the speed of the incoming tide, he would be in the neighborhood of the frigate in thirty minutes. He hoped she would be somewhere under his starboard side. But it was possible she would come under his larboard, for after a drift of two miles the brig might be brought closer inshore than he reckoned.

He would man both his larboard and starboard batteries, then. And thirty minutes after he got under way —perhaps twenty-five minutes if the flow of the tide were faster than he had looked for—he would fire both broadsides. Then he would reload immediately and fire again. The little eight-pounders, double shotted, were effective up to a mile and a half. The broadsides would sweep the sea a mile and a half on either side of the brig. There was a good chance that he would hit the frigate. He might even damage her heavily if he passed at close quarters. It was well worth the effort.

The brig was brought to anchor while the boat crews came back on board, and the gun crews went to their station. Now the cartridges were brought up from the powder hold and served out to the gunners who put them down the muzzles of their cannon, rammed a wad behind them, then inserted two eight-pound shot and rammed another wad behind these to keep the shot close to the cartridges. The wrappings were taken off the touchholes, and the slow fuses in the tubs beside each gun lit. It was all done without chatter. The crew had no concept of why they had been summoned to action stations in a fog so thick that no enemy could possibly sight them. Fore- and mainsail were brailed up to their yards, which was another preparation for action, increasing what little visibility there was on deck. Then the master gunner, the man with no teeth and a persistent thirst, reported to Peace of God that the guns were served and ready.

"Pass the word to the gunners to fire only on my command. Both broadsides," said Peace of God. "Then reload and fire again and reload once more and hold fire unless we are attacked. If attacked, let each gun on the side attacked fire as smartly as may be."

"Aye, aye, sir," said the master gunner. "And the target?"

"There is no target."

The master gunner raised a stubby forefinger and dug vigorously in his right ear, as if trying to get rid of some impediment in the ear passage. He had taken a quick nip of rum and water before coming on deck because of the thirst that was always on him, and he wondered whether he ought to have taken a little more water and a little less rum.

"You said no target, sir?" he asked.

"No target," repeated Peace of God.

"Elevation?" asked the master gunner.

"Five degrees," said Peace of God.

"No target. Five degrees elevation," repeated the master gunner and went off to give the orders. Back from him through the swirls of fog, came the remark, "Sea gulls."

Esek Hawkins, his thin, tall, dark-skinned first lieutenant, was standing beside Peace of God. Peace of

God knew little of this man who never talked of his background, living in a world of his own as if he had cut himself off from his fellow men because they were of no help or use to him in whatever were his troubles. He was a silent officer but extremely efficient. But he was also a mystery. Peace of God turned to him now.

"Pass the word to send two of the best men into the topmasts as lookouts," he said.

The lieutenant turned to give the order, and when he came back, Peace of God decided that the time had come to let his officers in on the details of his plan. He summoned them to his cabin—Hawkins, the first lieutenant, Luke Clemens, a stout, big-bellied man in his mid-fifties, the second lieutenant, and Tom Lears, the sailing master, who was responsible for the navigation of the ship under the captain's direction. He told them his plans briefly and then closely watched Hawkins. It was from him particularly that he wanted a reaction. But he got none. Hawkins remained silent, though the others grunted their approval. Peace of God felt disappointed. He had hoped to get some encouragement from Hawkins in this venture and he might as well have been talking to a stone wall.

"Any comments?" he asked.

The others gave a few words of approval, and Tom Lears, who was the youngest, even sounded excited and happy. But Hawkins did not even bow his head.

"What do you think, Mr. Hawkins?" asked Peace of God.

The others looked at him stonily. It was not a hostile look but it was a look quite without any emotion.

"I have no suggestions, sir," he said.

"You know your duty, then," said Peace of God. "Lieutenant Lears, take the starboard battery, and Lieutenant Clemens the larboard. And Lieutenant Hawkins, do thou stand by me at the poop to transmit orders and take command if aught befall." It was proper that he should have Hawkins with him as the first lieutenant. But Peace of God knew also that he wanted to observe the man under battle conditions and see if then he showed any kind of emotion.

Back on deck Peace of God gave the order to weigh anchor. The anchor had been put out over the stern so that the brig lay in the current of the tide, headed in the direction in which she was to go. As soon as he felt the brig move, he marked the time on his big watch by the light of a dark lantern. At anchor, the current running past the *Hornet* had produced a tinkling and gurgling sound. But now, moving with the current, the brig went forward without any sea noise, pushing into the wall of fog ahead and having the fog close in behind, so that there was no sense of traveling at all, apart from a slight rocking on the quiet water.

The gunners stood to their pieces, their positions marked only by the glowing of the slow matches over the sides of the tubs. The brig's canvas hung drearily upon her yards. Whatever wind there was, was from the west, and they were moving faster than it, so it had no effect on the sails. All was quiet and seemingly unreal.

In the silence there came, from above, a slight flap which quickly died away. Peace of God glanced upward and saw that the fore royal had filled for a moment and then collapsed. There was a little wind, then, a cat's-paw, a hundred feet above the surface of the Channel. It was a freak local wind but its significance was immediately apparent. The wind up there, if it increased, might disperse the top of the fog. The frigate's topmasts were higher by thirty feet than those of the brig. A sharp lookout on the *Cerebus* might sight the tops of the *Hornet*'s masts moving down on her through the fog and the surprise would be lost.

Peace of God was still watching the fore and main royals and saw that they were half filling and then collapsing. It was a fitful wind. It would stir the top of the fog back around, clearing one place and piling the fog up in the other, like a disorderly housewife pretending to sweep a room.

All would be well—if God willed it so.

He turned to his watch and was surprised that only five minutes had passed since weighing anchor. There were twenty-five to go, then—twenty-five minutes during which he could do nothing but wait. He did not mind waiting. The life of a fisherman was almost all patience and waiting. But he disliked being idle, which left the mind vacant and open to the suggestions of the devil. He should occupy himself with some godly exercise and so he thought on the prophecies of Jeremiah, who was his favorite of the biblical prophets, and the verse that came to his mind was from the sixth chapter, "Arise and let us go up in the night, and destroy her houses."

⚓ 46 ⚓

He said these words aloud, for that was his habit.

Hawkins heard him but made no comment. Lears, the youngest of the lieutenants, came back to the poop, picking his way rather clumsily across the deck.

"Davis on number-one gun reports hearing a noise to starboard," he said.

"What kind of a noise?" asked Peace of God.

"Splashing, sir," said Lears. "It might be someone rowing."

Might be a British picket boat, thought Peace of God. And it might be a fisherman letting out a net. Suddenly the lookout on the main topmast hailed the deck.

"Rocket ahead," he shouted. "Two points off the larboard."

"How far away?" yelled Peace of God.

"Hard to say," replied the lookout. "Might be half a mile."

Peace of God looked at his watch again. They had been under way twenty minutes. If they were on course, they would be within half a mile of the frigate. The rocket plainly came from her. She must be sending up rockets to recall her picket boats; to guide them back.

The lookout had reported the rocket ahead and to the larboard. If he maintained his present course, then, he would pass on the shoreward side of the frigate. He was about to hail the lookout again when the man in the fore maintop shouted, "Rocket ahead. To starboard. Three points off the bow."

"How far?" roared Peace of God.

⚓ 47 ⚓

"Half a mile, I'd say," replied the lookout. "It's dying out now."

Two rockets. One to larboard and one to starboard. Did that mean two frigates? Or were the lookouts up there in the fog confused about which was larboard and which starboard? A real seaman wouldn't become confused. But there were many green hands aboard the *Hornet*.

Peace of God turned to Hawkins. "What do you make of it, Mr. Hawkins?" he asked.

"Two frigates."

"I think you are right," said Peace of God. "A picket boat down in the gloom of the fog could not see a rocket. They are trying to find each other in the fog. One must be dragging her anchor and fearful she will come down upon the other. Well, I do not want to help them, but rather to hinder them. Send up a rocket of our own, Mr. Hawkins."

The rocket roared up from the deck, making an appalling brightness for a moment in the walls of fog around. It was immediately answered by two further rockets, one to larboard and one to starboard, both close enough to be seen as little smudges of light to left and right of the brig. The one to larboard was the nearest and was almost directly on the beam.

"Larboard broadside stand by to fire," roared Peace of God through his trumpet.

"Broadside ready," came back the voice of Lieutenant Clemens.

"Fire," roared Peace of God, and the slow matches

came down in little red arcs on the touchholes of the guns. The side of the brig blossomed red jets of flame which were baffled in the fog, giving the impression that the fog itself had caught fire.

"Starboard broadside stand by," Peace of God shouted.

"Starboard broadside ready," came back the excited voice of Lieutenant Lears.

"Fire!" roared Peace of God, and again the jets of flame spurted from the side of the *Hornet,* and the fog seemed for a moment enveloped in flame. When the high crack of the pieces had died away, there was a deathly silence aboard the brig, broken by the coughing of the gunners, for the smoke from the discharge did not clear away, there being no wind, and it was acrid and irritating to the lungs.

"Larboard broadside ready," shouted Lieutenant Clemens, who had been hustling his men to get their pieces recharged.

"Starboard broadside ready," cried Lears, and this time he was so excited that his voice was piping, like that of a boy of eight or ten.

Suddenly there was an immense explosion on the seaward side of the *Hornet.* It was as if a volcano had suddenly erupted in the sea, belching fire and thunder. This was immediately followed by roaring sounds which seemed to fill the air around. The main yard came tumbling to the deck, followed by the backstay. The broadside from the *Cerebus* made the little *Hornet* reel for a moment in the water. There was no need to order the *Hornet*'s gunners to reply. They did so immediately, the double-shotted eight-pounders barking sharply like angry terriers.

"Let go the stern anchor," Peace of God roared, and then, because he was not sure that the order, in the confusion, would be carried out fast enough, he pulled the pawl out of the capstan, and the anchor plunged into the sea. He was now anchored broadside to the *Cerebus* (if the seaward frigate were the *Cerebus*), and he was heartened to see a look of mild surprise on the face of Hawkins.

He gestured to the main yard lying smashed on the deck, and Hawkins immediately understood. To hit the main yard with her broadside, the British frigate could be scarcely more than two hundred yards away. Otherwise her shot would have gone high over the brig's mast. But at that range the *Hornet*'s broadsides would be hitting the frigate's hull, her guns being closer to the water. The frigate might dismast the *Hornet*, but she was unlikely to hole her.

Then, from the starboard side of the *Hornet*, there came another explosion, and the fog was illuminated suddenly and beautifully with yellow light. The second British frigate had joined the battle, and the *Hornet* was between the two of them.

"Cease fire," shouted Peace of God, but the words were drowned in another salvo from the second frigate. He grabbed Hawkins by his coat and, pulling his head down, roared the order in his ear, and the first lieutenant ran along the line of guns passing the order on.

So far the damage to the *Hornet*'s rigging was superficial. A few spars carried away and sheets and braces cut. The backstay was gone but, there being no wind, the mainmast was not endangered. But suddenly the bowsprit went, and the fore-topmast raked forward and then came toppling to the deck in a tangle of rigging.

The sailing master was on the wreckage immediately with a cleanup crew, hacking the tangle of rigging away and lashing the spars to the gunwales for possible use later.

It was time to move out of the cross fire. Peace of God had anchored so as to get the two British frigates firing into each other in the fog. They were doing that now and there was no purpose in remaining between them until masts and rigging were gone and the *Hornet* just a hulk. There was no time to bring the anchor in. Peace of God let the chain reel off the capstan drum and fall into the sea, and the brig moved off with the tide. The frigates were still hammering away at each other as he slipped from between them, and he told Hawkins to make an inspection of the brig and report any damage.

"What course?" asked Hawkins.

"Make as much northing as you can," said Peace of God. "Put a man on the lead line and report the first show of gray mud on the bottom."

Gray mud would mean that he was being swept up on the coast by the tide with two angry British frigates looking for him. Technically they could not come into the three-mile limit after him. But British naval officers had been known to sneeze at the letter of the law before. It would be better not to put them to the test.

⚓ 51 ⚓

He hoped the fog would hold long enough to let him get away. The frigates were still firing at each other, but they would discover their error any minute now, and then the hunt would be on. But he had reason to be satisfied with his night's work. Peace of God was a modest man, but he knew that the news of what he had achieved would create a storm of its own in England and France.

5

The Earl of Sandwich was making one of his rare appearances in the House of Lords, in his capacity as Lord of the Admiralty. He was a dissolute man and a degenerate one. He was so addicted to gambling that rather than tear himself away from the dice table to eat, he had his butler bring him a slice of meat between two slices of bread. This odd repast, under the name of a sandwich, was to be his only contribution to civilization, though the earl at the time was not aware of this. Command of the whole British Navy in the war against the American Colonies lay with him, and he had been informed by his secretary on awaking that morning that there was the devil to pay in the House of Lords over the recent incident in the Channel in which an American brig had simultaneously attacked two of His Majesty's frigates, causing them to fire on each other and slipping off itself comparatively unscratched.

His lordship was lying in bed when the news was brought to him of the uproar in the House of Lords.

"The devil to pay you say?" he commented. "Well, I had expected to pay him, though not in this life. However, since you assure me that he presents his bill, though before settlement is due, I shall attempt to meet it."

His lordship might be a rake and a drunkard and have all the fashionable vices of a corrupt age but he had one virtue and that was courage. And so he arose from his bed and dressed with care and had a glass of wine for his breakfast and now lounged in his seat in the House of Lords before his angry fellow peers, listening to the abuses they poured on his head.

The Earl of Adlington had the floor. He was a Chathamite—a man who before the war had favored the American cause and who now took every opportunity to criticize the king's ministers on their conduct of the war.

"We have arrived," he said, "at the very ebb of England's fortunes through the corruption of His Majesty's ministers. I ask you, my lords, to look around the scene and decide for yourselves whether the country has ever been so poorly served or has ever embarked upon so miserable a venture.

"The British Army and the British fleet have been

driven out of the city of Boston—that very city and port which it was the determination of His Majesty's ministers to humble and bring to its knees as the spawning ground of what was called treason and rebellion.

"The army of General Washington, scarcely a year ago, crossed the Delaware and inflicted a dual defeat on our own forces first at Trenton and then at Princeton. And that at a time when General Sir William Howe had assured the House that he had Washington trapped and would shortly exterminate his forces and bring an end to these troubles. Trapped, indeed! We cannot afford to set such traps which spring upon ourselves and set the whole of Europe laughing at us.

"Two months have hardly passed since we have had the black news of the surrender of General Burgoyne with the whole of his army at Saratoga in the Hudson Valley. There was another trap, my lords, which Burgoyne was to spring and which we were all assured would sever the northern American Colonies from their southern allies. I do not recall a single occasion in the present century where a British Army has had to surrender to the enemy. But that is what has taken place in America.

"And now we have the latest disaster in this litany of disasters. An American sloop of war, the brig *Hornet,* according to our agents, slips out of Le Havre and engages, not another sloop of war or an armed merchantman for which she might have been a match, but two British frigates, the *Cerebus* and *Staghound,* each of them mounting thirty-two guns.

⚓ 55 ⚓

"I ask you to reflect upon this, my lords, and by reversing the situation, perhaps come to some clearer understanding of the enormity of this triumph for our enemies and disaster for ourselves.

"I ask you to pretend, for the moment, that this sloop of war, the *Hornet* (most aptly named) was in the king's service. I ask you to suppose that we were at war with France. I ask you to pretend for the while that this sloop of war had the temerity to engage two French frigates and inflict such damage upon them that one had to return to port for a refit and the other, her cable cut, drifted up on the shore and could not be refloated without jettisoning half her guns.

"Would not we in England hail this as a tremendous feat of daring and of seamanship? Would not the bells ring in all our cities, the bonfires be lighted in our streets? The very pretense lifts our hearts with pride.

"But the *Hornet,* my lords, was an *American* vessel, and the frigates, His Majesty's ships. And such is the state of the navy under the administration of his lord-ship (gesturing to the lounging Earl of Sandwich) that two English frigates are not a match for an American sloop of war, and our home waters around these islands are not safe from an American raider who came three thousand miles across the ocean in midwinter to engage us.

"What has my noble lord to say in answer to all this?"

If the Earl of Sandwich had framed a reply, he was given no immediate opportunity to deliver it. Hardly had Adlington seated himself than he was followed by another peer, a man of large commercial interests, demanding whether there was any plan to protect merchant shipping carrying cargoes to England from American raiders in the Channel. And he was followed by a third, pressing for the recall of "Black Dick" Howe from the American station to guard the English coast.

To all of these the Earl of Sandwich listened with a silence that was almost insolent. He let them roar at him and rant at him, and now and again he stifled a yawn behind a lace handkerchief and occasionally exchanged a word or two with Lord North, the head of the government and therefore his ally, who sat beside him. Indeed, his indifference was such that at the height of the tumult he reached in the brocaded pocket of his frock coat and took out an ivory card case. From this he extracted a pack of playing cards and commenced shuffling them as if preparing for a game.

When at last his fellow peers had roared themselves out, he rose languidly and said, "I hardly think the Admiralty can be charged with the responsibility for the loss of Boston, the surrender of General Burgoyne and whatever it was that happened at Trenton and Princeton—two small towns somewhat removed from the ocean." Then he sat down again, and the furor was renewed only louder than ever.

"Answer!" his fellow peers shouted at him. "You must answer, my lord!" He let them shout and then rose again, the card case still in his beautifully manicured hands.

"I can answer only to the incident concerning the two frigates," he said. "Your lordships must absolve me from guilt in the other matters raised.

"As for the two frigates, it cannot be held at all that the American raider had any great part in the affair. According to my information, the frigates fired upon each other in dense fog. It was indeed deucedly foggy, as your lordships will perhaps recall, and two linkboys would not serve to fetch me to my carriage from White's, for I could see neither of them at four paces. The fog then being of the thickest sort, the two frigates mistook each other for enemies and opened fire, and although the incident is perhaps lamentable, I do not see that it is a matter for panic."

"What enemies were these frigates expecting to find in the Channel, my lord?" asked the Earl of Adlington. "Were they expecting an American frigate? I had not heard the Americans had any frigates. Come, my lord, is not all this a pretense on your part, and is not the plain truth of the matter that the American brig fired upon the two frigates and then escaped, leaving them to fire into each other?

"What is known of the whereabouts of this American raider now? And what is the name of her captain? Is she still at large to raid our commerce and threaten our shores and perhaps bring about some other debacle of the same sort?"

"As for the name of her captain," said the earl, "I understand it is a remarkable name and one which may amuse you—in view of the violence which attended upon his presence. It is Peace of God Manly."

There was a titter of laughter in the chamber. "I thought that might amuse you, my lords," said the earl, gratified. "Where his brig is at the present moment, I do not know. Our agents are searching for it. It should be no great task to find the brig, for it seems that it must be now somewhere in the North Sea. While I make no pretense to any knowledge of navigation, I am assured that to return into the Channel the brig must pass through the Straits of Dover, for to round Scotland in midwinter is unthinkable in such a ship. It will be quite easy to overtake her as she comes through the Straits and capture or sink her.

"I would assure the House that one American sloop of war, at large in the North Sea, can hardly be taken as a threat to the commerce of these islands."

"What specific steps are being taken in the matter?" Adlington persisted.

The Earl of Sandwich gave a delicate shrug and looked at Lord North. Plainly whatever steps were being taken, the earl did not know about them and did not care to bother his head about them. He was becoming a little bored with the whole proceeding and was anxious to get away. Lord North then decided to take up the cudgels on behalf of the earl.

"The chamber may rest assured," he said, "that all units of the fleet in home waters have been appraised of the presence of this raider. It will be found and dealt with. I suggest that we adjourn and spend no more time upon this business which is a small incident and cannot possibly affect the future of the war."

At that moment there came a sharp loud grunt and

all turned to look at the Earl of Chatham, a huge collapsing balloon of flesh who sat wheezing in his seat opposite Lord North. His legs were so swollen with dropsy that they resembled tree trunks, and the congested veins stood out on these swollen legs through the silk stockings that encased them. His body was as swollen in proportion as his legs and his face—a great block of a face that still bore a trace of its former good looks—was red and lined with tiny purple veins.

This was the man who had defied the king in the cause of the people, the great spokesman for liberty who had brought about, singlehandedly, the repeal of the infamous Stamp Act, and who had labored to prevent the outbreak of a war between England and her Colonies only to be defeated by smaller minds anxious to placate an ambitious monarch.

He was dying now, and had for two years, according to popular report, been in a coma, bereft of intelligence. But dying or not, he still commanded more respect than any man in England and his one sharp grunt was sufficient to focus the attention of the lords upon him as he slouched and wheezed in his seat.

"Your lordships will pardon me that I am temporarily unable to rise to address you," he said. "But the weakness is of the body and not of the mind.

"The Prime Minister has assured us that the presence of this American raider in our waters is no threat to the trade or security of these islands. What are his credentials for making such a statement? What does he know of trade who has ruined our trade with the American Colonies from which the ports of Liverpool, Bristol,

Southampton and London derived much of their income? And what does he know of security whose whole policy has been the insecurity of war—a policy based upon a strife that must separate us forever from our kinsmen in America who claimed in their lands the liberties we fought for and cherish in our own?

"His lordship's policy has committed this government to the destruction of its trade and perhaps separation forever from those Colonies for which Wolfe died at Quebec and the immortal Hawke defeated the naval might of France at Quiberon Bay."

The earl's great head sank for a moment forward on his chest. He remained in that position for some little while, sucking the air into his lungs in wheezes that could be heard in all parts of the attentive chamber. With a great effort he raised his head again, the face now much redder than it had been. He coughed and put a swollen hand to his mouth to cover his spittle, and the men around him flinched.

"What has been done in the past," said Chatham after making a great struggle to recover the power of speech, "has been all bad. But what may be done in the future may be disastrous.

"Your lordships are right to be disturbed by the presence of this American raider—this small American vessel, lightly armed and captained by a man called Peace of God. For he has demonstrated to the French that that of which they are most afraid—the strength of our fleet—may be nothing more than a phantom.

"They remember Quiberon Bay when Hawke engaged them in the teeth of a gale and shattered them completely. They remember when Hawke brought three hundred French prizes into English ports, and six thousand French sailors jammed English jails.

"These memories have kept them from siding with the Colonies in their revolt. But now will they not be asking themselves whether matters have not changed? Will not they look on the tremendous triumph of this little American vessel over two of our frigates? And will they not decide that they have been fearful of shadows and there is nothing now to stop them attaining that revenge upon us for which they have thirsted for over twenty years?

"My lords, we are unhappily at war with our Colonies. That war cannot be called off with honor on their part nor won with honor on ours. But a few more victories by the Americans in the field, and a few more raids by this brig, the *Hornet,* on our doorstep, and we may find ourselves not merely fighting our Colonies, but fighting France allied with our Colonies.

"It is in the face of this prospect that the Prime Minister seeks to assure us that the presence of the American raider in our home waters can have no effect on the future of the war."

When he had finished speaking, the earl attempted to rise and was helped to his feet by two menservants who stood behind his chair. He leaned heavily on them, glaring at Lord North across the chamber, and Lord North, stung out of his usual calm, shouted at him, "And what would you advise in these circumstances, my lord?"

"Advise?" said Chatham. "Find the *Hornet* and exterminate her, sir." And with that he shuffled out of the chamber. His departure marked the close of the debate. Their lordships dispersed about their affairs, much discomforted but attempting to assure each other that France would not attempt an alliance with the revolting Colonies.

Only the Earl of Sandwich seemed undisturbed. He waited, shuffling his pack of playing cards, until the chamber had cleared and then he himself left. Two liveried footmen greeted him as he gained the street. One opened the door of his carriage. The other produced a stool upholstered in red velvet and placed it upon the pavement. His lordship placed a slippered foot upon it and entered his carriage. The footmen closed the door and mounted hastily upon the platform at the back of the carriage, and immediately a mob of idlers closed around the vehicle shouting, "Jerry Twitcher. Jerry Twitcher."

It was the name of contempt they had for him. It referred to a tic that occasionally afflicted him after a period of excess which caused the corner of his mouth to twitch. The earl looked mildly out the window, as if examining a pleasant prospect rather than an angry mob. The coachman whipped up the team of matched horses, and the carriage lumbered off.

Soon the crowd had dispersed except for one man who leaned against a wall and was curiously engaged in cutting patterns out of a piece of paper with a pair of scissors.

6

The Continental brig *Hornet*, which had caused the uproar in the House of Lords, lay at anchor off the island of Texel, the first of a string of low-lying islands that formed a seaward fence, as it were, around the coast of Holland. It was four days after the engagement of the frigates *Cerebus* and *Staghound* off Le Havre, and Peace of God had taken the *Hornet* to Texel to do a better job on the repairs to her rigging than he had been able to contrive at sea. The bowsprit provided the most concern. It had been sheered off ten feet from the bow. The ship's carpenter had jury-rigged a temporary bowsprit to bring the brig to Texel. But a completely new bowsprit was needed, as well as a main yard for the foremast. It would take him a week to refit, and Peace of God was disturbed about his situation.

The island of Texel was little more than a sand bar of vast extent rising out of the ocean. There was no spot on it more than twenty feet above the water at high tide. When the tide went out, the area of the island was doubled, for the receding waters exposed an enormous portion of the sea bed to the east and north of the island so that what at high tide looked like the sea, at low tide was a desert of water-soaked sand stretching to the horizon.

When the tide came in, it advanced as a white line of foam, rushing with astonishing speed over this exposed sea bottom. It brought a noise with it, a deep roar full of wrath. The advancing sea leaped in plumes and columns over the sand where two or three streams of the tide would meet. All was wild and ugly at such times. It was appalling to see, four miles away, the tide come sweeping in like a charge of cavalry over the sands. There was always a cluster of birds over the incoming tide, herring gulls and terns. They whirled above it like chips of wood or leaves in a gust of wind, snapping at the little fishes that were swept in by the tide.

The *Hornet* lay, at low tide, on her beam ends, tied up to a rickety, stinking dock at Oosterend, on Texel. When the tide was full, she floated. But when it went out, she settled on her side, her timbers groaning under the pressure and her masts raked out over the water.

⚓ 65 ⚓

At low tide, the *Hornet* looked like a stranded wreck. When the rushing millrace of the tide returned, the *Hornet* rolled uneasily on the bottom in the swirling water, shifting upright inch by inch, her planks straining, her masts shivering and her rigging taut as fiddle strings.

Peace of God suffered to see his brig four times a day subjected to this ordeal. He could feel her travail; sense the strain on her when the whole weight of the brig was put on the few planks of one side that rested on the bottom. But there was no help for it. Refit he must, and Texel, he had been told by Dr. Franklin, was a good place to do this.

Certainly he believed he was safe from the British, lying on the shoreward side of the gloomy flat sand bar of an island. They dare not bring a frigate into such uncertain water. There was only one deep passage from the open sea to the landward side of the island called the *stroom*.

In this channel the depth varied from an uncertain ten to forty feet between tides. The channel was like a millrace when the tide was flowing or ebbing. No frigate dared attempt that passage, and the Hollanders themselves attempted it only during the half hour of slack water between tides.

Peace of God had other worries besides the situation of his ship and the need for repairs. One of them was his crew. It was impossible for them to live aboard with the ship being rolled over on her side and then upright with each tide, and so they had taken quarters ashore among the fishermen in Oosterend. And Simmons, the master gunner, had been intoxicated most of the time. There was no way to keep the man sober and he would be useless for a couple of days after getting to sea. The rest of the crew who were not busy with repairs were idling on the island. Idling was bad for them. It provided an opportunity for the devil to lay snares to trap them. To combat the wiliness of this voracious arch-enemy of all mankind, Peace of God called a prayer meeting morning and evening every day in a little square in the village. He invited his crew to be present at these prayer meetings and because there was not very much else to do they attended.

"Ah, poor sinners all," he would say, "consider how we are held snug here on the leeward side of the hand of God, as it were, protected from the storm of the ocean and the fogs and winds and tides and all manner of hazards that attend life at sea. Look around you and see the goodness of God and reflect upon it. Every man well fed and housed and sheltered from the winter's blast. Ship provisioned and repairs going forward in a seamanly manner, though do thou, Sam Peters, as ship's carpenter, look better to the seating of the bowsprit butt. It will not do fastened to the foot of the foremast but must be lodged securely against the keel. For a bowsprit is like faith in the Lord and cannot be made to depend upon any uncertain foundation or in time of stress it will be certain to carry away . . ."

"If the bowsprit is lodged on the keel 'twill increase her steeve and she will rake up so high she will fight her helm going to windward," interrupted the ship's carpenter.

"It's a samson post I am talking of, Sam Peters, as you well know," replied Peace of God. "A good oak samson post set in the keel, fastened to the foot of the foremast with dowels and metal straps and the bowsprit butted into it. But you know this well and are a sinner like myself and will find five ways to do a thing wrong when what is needed is but one way to do it right.

"But the right way is the hard way and always will be, for sinners that we are, we were put here to struggle might and main toward righteousness. We must tear ourselves away from the lee shore of evil and laziness where the land looks pleasant but is full of reefs and shoal water, and clear our way to seaward to the rocky island of righteousness, though our hands be bleeding from rough uses at sheets and braces and our muscles ache and our bones crack and our feet be blue with the cold.

"Claw off we must and if we do there will come a time when the seas will quieten and the wind come gentle and God will send his angel to take us into the harbor of glory, and all our strife with topsails carried away and contrary winds and fouled gear will be at an end, amen.

"And now, sinners all, let us join in a hymn of praise to our Creator."

Peace of God's hymns were set to the tune of chanteys, a favorite being "The Amsterdam Maid," a capstan chantey for which he had substituted appropriate words. The crew did not mind the change. A rousing song is a rousing song and will cheer a man on a gloomy day and brisken his work. They would join in with gusto, singing the praises of the Lord to the tune that once sang the praises of the maid of Amsterdam and roaring the amended chorus that now went:

"We'll go no more a-roving, from you, dear Lord."

The people of the island attended these prayer meetings of the brig's captain and were impressed by them. They did not understand why Peace of God did not join them in their houses in the evening for a glass of gin or rum and a pipe of tobacco as the rest of the ship's company did. But they respected him enormously both for his engagement with the two British frigates and his stern devotion to his religion.

When he had been at Texel only a couple of days, his influence had spread all over the island. The people accepted the crew and the officers as their own. But they looked up to Peace of God with respect, and when he visited a house, the rum and gin were put aside and the pipes of tobacco also, and the people listened to him talk of the need for salvation.

The islanders, fishermen all, for there was nothing to farm on Texel, spoke, besides their native Dutch, French and English. They were not fluent in these tongues but had a working knowledge of them because they shared fishing grounds with French and English fishermen.

Their boats were of shallow draft, very beamy and fitted with leeboards. The biggest of them drew but three feet of water, for otherwise they would not be able to sail over the innumerable sand bars around their island. But friendly as the islanders were, Peace of God was still worried. Nothing would prevent them telling other fishermen of the advent of the *Hornet*. The word would get around in time to French fishermen and English too. In short, it would not be long before the fact that the *Hornet* lay off Texel was known to the British fleet, and the hunt for him would be concentrated around Dutch waters.

There was nothing he could do about this, however, but hurry the work of repairs forward and hold his prayer meetings as a safeguard against idleness, and to fret every time the tide let the brig down on her beam ends and then, returning, raised her again.

The weather had, in the meantime, turned clear and bitterly cold. A scouring wind flung out of the northeast, bringing the sharp bite of frost with it. The whole island each morning was coated with frost, which even powdered the sand of the beach. The howling wind whipped the inflowing tide over the sand flats into an appalling wild area of foam.

The day before the repairs were finished, the glass fell heavily and it was apparent that a full gale was approaching. The *Hornet* then would be delayed and there was the more time for news of her presence to reach the British fleet.

The only consolation lay in the fact that with the repairs completed, the brig could be taken into deeper water, though still within the harbor, where she could float at all stages of the tide. Her ballast, which had been taken out during the repairs and coated with pitch, was restored and the crew ordered back aboard. The gale, the islanders predicted, would last for a week; perhaps ten days.

Every morning Peace of God went ashore taking a glass with him and fought his way in the teeth of the wind to the seaward side. There he examined the murky wind-stricken ocean for sight of a frigate which he was sure would not be long finding his hiding place.

He sighted the frigate on the third day of the gale. She lay out in the welter of the sea under fore-topgallant, forestaysail and spanker. She was hove to, clawing into the wind, and all that could be seen of her was her masts with the rags of sail on them dark against the gray sky. The silent Hawkins had accompanied Peace of God across the island, and the sight of the frigate, her decks awash, still keeping the sea, moved him to speech.

"She'll be the *Cerebus*," he shouted above the wind. There was a touch of admiration in his voice. "Unless the *Cerebus* carries away her topmasts in the gale, we are as good as prisoners," he added. "The *Cerebus* will block the *stroom*—the only channel by which we can gain the North Sea. We will be bottled up in here for the rest of the war."

"Yet I mean to get out, God willing," said Peace of God.

The next day and the day after, the frigate was still at her post, standing off and on. She closed up the seaward entrance of the *stroom* channel as effectively as a cork closes a bottle. A night escape was impossible. The channel was scarcely forty yards wide at its broadest.

On both sides were sandbanks, and there were two or three shifting bars of sand in the center. A pilot would have to have daylight to get the *Hornet* safely to sea, and the frigate would see her coming and sink her with one broadside. When, on the fifth day of the gale, the frigate was still in position, Peace of God fell to studying his charts. They were not good charts. They did, however, show the vast shoals to the north and east of the island which was called the *Waard Granden* and which were uncovered at low tide. At high tide there was a dubious ten feet of water over these sands and then for only a couple of hours. When the tide ebbed, the water drained off at an enormous pace. The *Hornet* drew twelve feet. So even with the fullest flood tide, there was still not enough water to sail the brig over the *Waard Granden*.

But there was one aspect of the chart that now interested Peace of God. It showed a potential channel, once the narrowest part of the shoal area had been cleared. It was called the *Engleschmangat*.

"The Englishman's gate," one of the fishermen told him, when he consulted him about the chart. "There was an English ship in here many years ago and she got out over the shoal sands at high tide and through the channel. And that is how it got its name."

"She could not have been a big ship, then," said Peace of God.

"She was a bigger ship than yours," said the islander.

"How did she get over the shoal?" asked Peace of God.

"Ah, those English," replied the islander. "They live in the sea like fish and know all the tricks. He used barrels."

"Barrels?"

"Yes. He drew fourteen feet of water. Well, he lightened the ship of her cargo and that raised her a foot in the water. But he was still three feet too deep. Then, he lashed barrels along her sides—empty, watertight barrels. And that raised her another two feet. So he was still one foot too deep. Then he threw out his ballast and that raised her two feet. And so he got over the shoal and into the channel. And then he anchored and took on ballast in the channel and got to sea."

"There are plenty of barrels on the island?" asked Peace of God.

"There are plenty. We use them for packing salted herring. But I wouldn't try the Englishman's trick if I were you. He had fair weather and an offshore wind. You have the wind foul and blowing a gale, and if the tide leaves you on the sands, your ship will be broken up in twenty-four hours."

"Nonetheless I will try the barrels," said Peace of God.

He was two days making what amounted to a floating dock to take the *Hornet* over the shoals. Forty barrels, twenty to a side, were lashed together with a sling of ropes between them like a netting.

This sling was made short so that when the brig was put in it, the barrels would be submerged and would raise the vessel four feet higher in the water than she

⚓ 73 ⚓

floated normally. To lighten the brig further he dumped two tons of ballast, substituting for this the cannon shot he had taken on in Le Havre.

If he got into a hot engagement, he would, by shooting his ballast overboard, lighten the ship with every broadside and make her cranky and unseaworthy. But he hoped to be able to take on stone ballast once he got away from the frigate.

His guns he would not part with. If he dumped them, the ship would be lightened so as to rise another foot in the water. But without her guns she was useless for service. So the guns stayed and on the morning of the eighth day of the gale, which showed no signs of abating, he was ready for the attempt.

The day before, at low tide, and despite the fury of the wind, Peace of God had gone out on foot over the shoal area over which he must sail at the flood. He took a compass with him and a chart and on this sketched in a series of bearings which would give him the maximum depth when he made his attempt.

At eight the following morning he was ready. The wind being from almost dead ahead, he could set no sails, and in any case sails would be of little help, for the brig was made clumsy by the girdle of barrels on which she floated.

At seven, before it was light, he had heard the tide start roaring in over the shoals. It came from two directions, sweeping through the *stroom*. These two streams would meet in the middle of the shoal in a turmoil of water which would throw the brig around mercilessly.

He must, however, be well on to the shoal area by that time.

There was but twenty minutes of full tide and then the waters would start to recede, slowly at first, but accelerating with every minute. By the time the ebb started he must be past the middle of the shoal—the divide—so that the outflowing sea would pull him along to the Englishman's gate. If he were in the dead center, he would be stranded. If he were south of the center, his best hope would be to retreat with the tide to Oosterend to make the attempt once more with the next flood.

Having then no sail on the brig, he had to tow her through the water with boat crews. He employed two boats which went ahead with anchors. These they dropped when they were ten cable lengths ahead of the brig. Men at the capstan then hauled in on the anchors, pulling the brig forward. The system was known as kedging. It was a system for use in a flat calm. He was using it in a gale and a wild sea.

At eight it was still dark, and the boats ahead were invisible from the deck and were steering toward the shoal by compass. The tide was starting to run strongly, and the swirl of it could be heard around the brig. She tried to veer away from the boats, caught broadside by the tide. It was here that the anchors came in handy. Dropped, they held firmly in the sand, and the men at the capstan hauled in on them, heaving the brig in the darkness toward the shoals.

Flood tide would be by half past nine. By that time

⚓ 75 ⚓

the brig would have to be kedged a mile and a half onto the shoal to be over the divide when the ebb set in.

The problem was: Could the boats, in the darkness and the roaring sea, keep her on course? Or would the brig drag them to the westward where the sands expanded into a shoal area covering fifteen square miles and where she would be wrecked?

The next hour would decide the matter.

7

·
·
·
⚓

By nine o'clock an uncertain light had begun to steal
over the sands, and the lookout in the foretop of the
Hornet reported that he could at last see the boats
ahead. They were on course and getting a little shelter
from the gale under the lee of the island. But the rowers
were working in a terrible swirl of murky water which
made it difficult for them to keep their course.

At times they would be caught in a rip tide and
swept ten or fifteen feet out of their way in the same
number of seconds. There was a man standing in the
bow of each boat, spotting these rip tides and shouting

a warning to the helmsman. He, also standing, tried to apply the necessary correction but often was not in time, and the boat would be whirled away in the rip like a chip of wood in a gutter stream.

What kept the brig from being swept away also was the fact that there was always one anchor down while the other was being taken ahead to be dropped. But even so, she swung around on her anchor, at times was in danger of fouling her own cable, and her wheel spun crazily left and right, for there was no sense manning it.

When the light had increased a little, Peace of God went himself into the foretop to con the ship. Ahead lay a seething cauldron of water, waves and currents running in every direction as the tide flowed over the sandbanks, and the collision of these waves throwing up water spouts on all sides which he judged must be seven and eight feet high.

In the middle of this cauldron there was an area of sand which the tide had not yet reached. There were about two hundred yards of exposed sea bottom laced around by the tide. Spearheads of white water flickered over this, driven ahead of the tide by the wind. They would be there for a few seconds and then gone as the wind lifted them up into the air in driving spray.

Peace of God watched the exposed area carefully, shielding his eyes with his arm against the wind and foam which was flung even as high as the topmast. The exposed area was growing smaller by the minute. It was still three miles away and it would be submerged in an hour. Something had gone wrong with his calculations then. The tide was coming in much faster than he had reckoned, and by the time he got to the divide in the sands, it would have started to ebb. He would certainly be stranded unless he could hurry the brig forward.

Dickie, the powder boy, was in the foretop and secretly delighted to have Peace of God there also. It was Peace of God who had first sent him into the foretop shortly after they cleared Boston. Then he had been sick with fright, and Simmons, the master gunner, had had to come up and get him down.

But now he was perfectly at home and to show with what ease he could perch in the topmast, he was sitting on the royal yard and scorned to hold on to anything with his hands. Peace of God glanced at him and frowned. That was how youngsters got killed. They became overconfident and neglected to take a handhold when in the tops. A sudden jolt unseated them and hurled them to death on the deck below. So it was with all mankind, for men became confident of salvation, and taking no handhold in prayer and good works, were in an unguarded moment snatched into perdition.

He shouted to the boy to come in off the yard and get an arm around the topmast. The boy grinned but pretended not to hear. Peace of God beckoned. The boy remained where he was, grinning. He even folded his arm on his chest, so that his only perch was the contact between his rump and the slim pole of the yard.

Peace of God grasped the sling of the royal yard with one hand, stepped out on the yard itself, and with the other hand grabbed the boy under the arm. A second later a tremendous shudder shook the whole brig. Topmast and yard whipped violently back and forth, and the boy was flung off the yard and hung dangling over the deck held only by the grasp Peace of God had upon his arm. The captain retained his footing on the yard and his hold on the sling, but he could feel the boy falling away from him by fractions of an inch as his coat slipped through his grasp.

There was but one thing to do—swing the boy outward toward the rigging of the topgallant yard below. It was impossible to haul him up. There was no time to explain to the boy either. He swung him outward and then with a prayer released his hold. The boy gave a scream and then, like a monkey, clutched at the sling of the topgallant, slipped a few inches, clutched again, and finally held fast and lowered himself to the topgallant yard.

As soon as the boy was safe, Peace of God looked around to see what had caused the shock. He found that the brig, her masts caught in an especially fierce gust of wind, had slewed to the westward and struck on a sand bar. The men at the capstan were trying to haul her off but were incapable of budging her. With a rising tide, she would come off in time. Fifteen minutes at the latest should see her free. But he had not fifteen minutes to spare. She must be hauled free immediately so that he would be out over the center of the shoal at flood tide and not be left there as the waters receded.

Normally he would return to the deck by the ratlines but the need now was for speed. He hooked a leg over the fore-topmast backstay and slid down this, hand over hand, reaching the deck in a matter of seconds.

⚓ 80 ⚓

"Does she budge?" he roared at Hawkins who was standing by the straining men at the capstan.

"No," shouted Hawkins. "She's dragging her anchor and sucking into the sand."

"Is the other anchor down?"

"Aye," replied Hawkins.

"Pass the line to the capstan aft and heave on both anchors," snapped Peace of God. "Master Gunner," he continued, "heave those starboard guns amidships. Lively now. See there are hammocks handy." The hammocks would be needed to block the wheels of the gun carriages. The guns, once released from their lashings, would charge around the deck with each roll of the vessel, maiming and killing men unless hammocks were used to block their wheels.

When the guns were hauled to the center of the deck, and the forward and aft capstans manned to heave on both anchors, the brig inched reluctantly forward until at last, in a swirl of murky water, she broke free of the slough of sand into which she had blundered. Peace of God now became conscious of something different about the wind. It had veered around a little to the west, and it was this change in direction that had flung the brig eastward onto the sand bar.

He went aft to the compass by the wheel and taking a bearing found that the wind was now coming from the northwest. It was a wind by which he could sail. He gave the order to set the topgallants and the forestaysail, the maximum of storm canvas he believed he could carry. The effect was immediate. The brig steadied in the water, and the helm now being manned, she responded to it and could be brought and held to a course toward the center of the shoal.

Here the sand no longer showed. The tide, flowing more swiftly around the island from the north because of the wind than from the south, had won the race and swept over the divide of the shoal. The whole area was a maelstrom of lashed and panicked water, into which the *Hornet* was now treading its way. The men in the boats were almost exhausted with their struggles. Their craft, handicapped by the need to pay out the anchor cable astern, would be hard to manage in a calm sea. In this witches' cauldron the boat spun around, swerved sideways, drifted downwind three feet for every four they made forward, and Peace of God sensed that the water would be up to the thwarts in the boats and bailing close to impossible.

"Make a signal to recall the boats," he said to Hawkins. "We'll go the rest of the way under sail."

Hawkins gave him a look of disbelief. Their only safety, their only guarantee of not being swept by tide and wind off to the east into the fifteen square miles of shoal water that lay under their lee, was in the anchors. With an anchor down, the brig could at least hold where she was. But with her anchors aweigh, any rip tide, and there were a score of them in the horrible water ahead, could sweep her away.

He shrugged and ordered the signals set, and the boats dropped their anchors for the last time and came alongside. Some of the men were so exhausted that they had to be helped aboard by their mates. They were soaked with brine, and the brine had frozen on the upper parts of their clothing which were more exposed to the wind. Here their jackets and jerseys were white with frost. The faces of some of the men were gray with exhaustion, and seeing them in this plight Peace of God swallowed one of his scruples for the moment.

"Boat crews below, Mr. Clemens," he said to that young officer who had been out in one of the boats. "See that they change clothes and give them two fingers of rum each. Then all hands on deck. I'll give you ten minutes."

"Aye, aye, sir," said Clemens with an attempt at a grin which was nothing more than a grimace, he was so weary. Meanwhile the starboard guns had been returned to their position and lashed there. Peace of God took one look up at the topgallants and went aft, taking the wheel of the brig himself.

"Put two men up in the foretop," he said to Hawkins, "and two men forward with lead lines."

The brig, because of her girdle of barrels, was extremely slow in answering her helm. Peace of God had spent forty years at sea and of that time perhaps as much as twenty years had been spent with a tiller or helm in his hands. He could feel a ship through her wheel, feel not only the sea under her hull but also the wind in her sails, and her trim in the water and what leeway she was making. He was always nervous when, at a time of crisis, someone else was at the wheel, for he felt himself cut off from those little messages about the ship's condition and behavior essential to him. So now, at the wheel of the *Hornet*, he felt more at ease and kept an eye on the luff of the main topgallant which would be the first to back if the brig were brought too close to the wind.

"By the mark two," sang out the leadsman. He had two fathoms of water then below him—twelve feet. Buoyed up by the barrels, the *Hornet* drew nine feet. He took a quick look at the compass and made a rough bearing on a point of land dimly seen in the scud ahead. He was in the very slight channel whose course he had worked out in his walk over the shoals the previous day. But the channel could readily shift under the scouring of the tide. He wished he could see the water ahead, for by the condition of the surface he could pick out the deeper areas. But back by the poop he could see nothing.

"White water one hundred yards off the starboard," yelled one of the lookouts, his voice coming only thinly to the deck though he was using a speaking trumpet.

"White water dead ahead," yelled the other lookout.

"Quarter less two," called the leadsman.

A sand bar lay ahead then. It shouldn't be but there it was—a sand bar perhaps created in a matter of minutes. He put the helm up, watching the main topgallant. The brig slewed slowly around in the water, inch by inch. The luff of the main topgallant started to tremble, and the brig came almost to a standstill. The barrels were slowing her down more than he had reckoned. He spun the wheel to leeward, watched the topgallants fill, felt the brig pick up speed and then drove her into the wind again. This time she came up more readily and by her own inertia moved a hundred feet through the water, the topgallants flapping furiously as if to tear themselves from the yards.

He had to get her off the wind again and spun the wheel. The sails filled with a crack, but the brig hardly moved. Then she picked up a little speed but not enough to suit him, and Peace of God knew there was something wrong.

Was she dragging her keel over the sand bar? Or were some of the submerged barrels touching bottom?

"Quarter less two," called the leadsman. Nine feet of water, thought Peace of God. She must be just on the bottom, just touching the sand. It was touch and go whether she stuck fast or fought free. He eased the helm downwind a trifle, so the sails would draw better and perhaps force her over the sandbank. For a moment the brig picked up speed. And then, as if she had sailed into a wall, she held fast, and the moment she struck, the men on deck were hurled staggering against the bulwarks by the impact.

There was no need to give the order to take the sails off her. Hawkins himself had sprung into the rigging, the topmen following him, and the two topgallants were furled in a matter of two minutes. Lears, meanwhile, the fat-bellied lieutenant, who had appeared on deck with his boat's crew, looked helplessly around. He was a slow man on the move and inclined to take a pessimistic view of everything. It was the young Lieutenant Clemens who tumbled his men into a boat and, taking an anchor with him, started to row upwind to deep water. He had the anchor out in five minutes, and the men had manned the capstan and were hauling in on it. It was a short haul. No more than thirty feet. But thirty feet, if it could be achieved, would take them off the sand bar.

Peace of God, nimble as a monkey despite his years, ran forward along the bowsprit whence he could not only see the water ahead but, looking back, see the hull of the brig and judge how badly she was stuck. He learned two things. Fifty feet ahead, no further than that, was the beginning of the channel, the Englishman's gate for which he was headed. And the brig, tilted over on her starboard side, was deeper in the water than she should be, buoyed up by the barrels. The reason was plain. Some of the barrels had been stove in. Of course they were stove in. He should have thought of that. They had been broken in the jolt that had nearly shaken the powder boy Dickie from the foretopmast yard. He had been so concerned about saving the youngster's life that he had forgotten about the possibility of damage to the barrels.

The brig would have to be kedged off. Only fifty yards to go and she would be in water in which she could sail. But he had taken far too long in arriving at this point. The tide was beginning to ebb. By the time he made that fifty yards the tide would have dropped another foot. He could not spare that foot of water, and the brig must be lightened.

"Jettison all but sea stores," he ordered Hawkins as he regained the deck. "Send out the other boat's crew to help kedge us off. Lively now. Half an hour and all is won or lost."

⚓ 86 ⚓

"What about the guns?" asked Hawkins.

"They stay aboard," said Peace of God grimly.

Soon a party of men were staggering out of the forecastle with sea chests, hammocks, bedding, clothing—all the possessions they could lay hands on—and dumping them over the side. Two hogsheads of water went along with four of salt pork. But the effect was negligible. The men at the capstan strained at the bars but could not heave in on the anchors.

"Cut us free of the barrels," Peace of God ordered. He was gambling that it was the barrels that were locked in the sand and the hull itself was free of it. The cables holding the barrels around the hull were cut off, and the brig moved forward perhaps four feet and then stuck fast again. There were two other devices that could be used, and if these failed, the *Hornet* could not be got off the sand.

"All hands not needed for duty get into the boats," Peace of God commanded. That might lighten the ship of the weight of forty men, each of the boats being capable of holding twenty. The boats, having set the anchors, had returned alongside, and the men tumbled into them, lightening the brig of perhaps a ton and a half. But the brig was still held by the sand, though she seemed on the point of moving.

One way left, then, to perhaps shake her loose.

"Fire the starboard broadside," Peace of God snapped at Simmons. The recoil of the guns might jerk the ship off the sand bar. Otherwise the guns themselves would have to be tumbled overboard as a last and desperate measure.

Simmons, the master gunner, was sufficiently recovered from his bout of drinking ashore to attend to
this personally. His hands were shaking and not from
cold as he went about the business, however. "Thou art
as close to a wreck, Master Simmons, as this vessel,"
said Peace of God to himself. "And I must save you or
answer to the Lord that I let you be driven upon a lee
shore."

Simmons tried to light a slow match with which to
touch off the guns, but they were damp as a result of
his carelessness. He stumbled into the galley and came
out with a hot coal in a pair of tongs. Peace of God
caught a glimpse of the boy Dickie's face. The youngster was standing near him by the break of the poop
and his face was white with fear, for he believed that
the ship would break up and they would be drowned.
The captain would have liked to comfort the lad but
there was no time. He looked up at the yards. The topmen were still there, ready to loose the topgallants if
the ship got free of the sand bar.

Simmons touched the coal to the touchhole of the
first of the guns, and it fired with a sharp crack, jerking
back against its lashings. It seemed to Peace of God
that the vessel moved an inch.

"Heave on those capstans," he shouted. "Heartily
now. All hands." He put a gnarled hand on the boy
Dickie's shoulder and pushed him forward toward the
capstan. The boy's fears would be less if he had something to do. The second gun barked, again the brig
shuddered, seemed to move, but remained firm. As
Simmons went to the third gun, blowing on his coal to

keep it alight, Peace of God went to the fourth. He pulled a pistol from his pocket where he had it wrapped in an oilskin to keep the priming dry. As Simmons touched the hot coal to the third gun, Peace of God fired the pistol over the touchhole of the fourth, holding it close so that the flame from the pan ignited the powder in the touchhole. Both guns went off simultaneously. This time there was no mistaking the effect. The brig slid a foot off the sandbank, hesitated a moment and then moved reluctantly toward her anchors while the men at the capstan drove forward on the bars, cheering in triumph.

And then from the lookout in the foretop came a thin cry of "Boats ahead in the channel."

The *Hornet* was still hedging off the shoals, and a British boat party from the frigate was coming down on them preparing to board.

8

Captain Sir Thomas Greenhow of His Majesty's frigate *Cerebus,* thirty-two guns, unlike most British naval captains of his day, was a man of wealth, who might, if he wished, have lived a life of ease ashore on vast country estates which occupied no small part of the county of Devon. He was the owner of a manor house at Tavistock and another outside Exmouth. These had been in his family for three hundred years. He had a town house near the Mall in London, forty blood hunters, five carriages and an income from his properties of a hundred and twenty thousand pounds a year.

A bachelor, aged thirty-two, he was then one of the most eligible men in England. The wits of the London clubs maintained that he had been driven to sea by the ambitious horde of women ashore who sought to entrap him in matrimony.

Others held that he was mad.

All the Greenhows had been mad. Sir Thomas' grandfather had spent his whole life wandering Europe, not with a court of his own following him about and living lavishly, but like a beggar or a packman, having no more than a few shillings in his pocket at one time.

It was common knowledge that he had been arrested in Venice as a vagrant and deported before the magistrates discovered that the man they took as a vagrant was actually one of the greatest and richest of the English nobility.

Sir Thomas' great-grandfather, sixty years previously, had joined a band of French explorers in Canada and had been killed by the Iroquois on the shores of Lake Erie. It was not surprising, then, that the present Sir Thomas, Earl of Tavistock, should turn his back on two manor houses, a town house and his vast estates, and live the life of a dog on the cramped quarters of the British frigate, manned by the sweepings of the London taverns.

All who knew Sir Thomas agreed on one point: He was the devil of a man to cross. At seventeen he had killed the son of a French envoy in a duel over some minor disagreement, and it had taken two thousand pounds to patch up the scandal. At eighteen, to settle a bet, he had ridden from Exeter to London in the unthinkably fast time of ten hours, killing four horses on the way. At nineteen he had swum a horse, himself on its back, across the Thames below London Bridge. At twenty he had mortally offended the Earl of Bute by calling upon him dressed in an ape's skin and hailing him as brother.

It was at this time that he had become fascinated with the sea and bought himself a commission as captain of a frigate. That he knew nothing of sailing did not disturb a corrupt Admiralty. He was assigned to his frigate and it was thought that in a matter of weeks he would tire of the venture and resign.

But Sir Thomas Greenhow did not tire of the venture. The hardship of life on a frigate—even for a captain—provided him with the challenge he seemed to have spent his youth looking for. He embraced the challenge, learned all he might of seamanship, served under Hawke at Quiberon Bay, sinking a French two-decker, stormed a fort on Corsica and spiked the guns, and later sank two Algerian corsairs off the Barbary coast.

In a navy that had been allowed to go to pieces following the defeat of the French, he was one of the few captains who was completely competent and anxious for a fight. His discipline was of the sternest and yet he was enormously popular with his men, for whatever hardship was theirs he shared himself. At sea he ate the same wormy ship's biscuits served to the forecastle hands, tapping them upon the table to shake out as many weevils as possible before biting off a piece.

This, then, was the man who had been assigned the

task of finding and exterminating the American brig *Hornet*, captained by someone with the unlikely name of Peace of God Manly.

His orders from the Admiralty were explicit.

"You will use the utmost vigilance in discovering the whereabouts of the brig *Hornet*," they read, "and immediately on sighting, engage her whatever the condition of the weather. The Admiralty is prepared to place at your disposal whatever units you wish, but their lordships are of the opinion that one frigate, especially under your command, should be sufficient for the task.

"Our agents suggest Texel as the possible hiding place of the *Hornet*. You will be approached by one of our agents at Le Havre who will give you the latest intelligence.

"If it is necessary to invade Dutch territorial waters to destroy the *Hornet*, you may be assured of our support."

So he had brought the *Cerebus* to Texel and for a week had stood on and off the island, waiting for the *Hornet* to emerge. And then, like Peace of God, he had started studying again the charts of the water around the island and seen the potential second avenue of escape through the *Engelschmangat*.

Would this captain from Salem attempt such an escape? Sir Thomas had barely posed the question before he knew the answer. Any man who in a fog would drift down on two frigates and fire into them was a man of sufficient daring and ingenuity to chance gaining the sea over the shoals.

But when?

Well, it didn't really matter when. The thing to do was to seal up the *Engelschmangat* with a boat party, and it was that party now that the topman on the *Hornet* had sighted in the wild channel ahead.

Sir Thomas was in the lead boat, the others (there were five all told) stringing out in the wild water behind. As soon as he heard the *Hornet* fire her guns, he knew that she was aground and struggling to get off the sand. He had her then. All that was necessary to do was to cut the cables to her anchors and she would run aground again, this time without hope of getting off. Then he could board her, fighting his way aboard if any resistance were offered and bring her as a prize into Portsmouth. He glanced at the twenty seamen heaving on the oars in the seats ahead of them. They were pulling with a will well used to boat work in rough water. Some had their cutlasses between their teeth. Others had them hung by a lanyard over their backs to be out of the way of the oars. They were all armed and would go into the fight like terriers in a pit.

He put the tiller over to head his boat for the *Hornet*'s anchor cables at the point where they entered the water and, turning, waved the other boats behind to head toward the brig itself. They could board her while his crew cut the anchor cables. Five minutes should see the cables cut. Fifteen minutes of fighting and then the brig would be his.

"Heave hearty," he shouted. "She's ours, by thunder! She's ours."

Aboard the *Hornet*, Peace of God had taken in the situation at a glance. He saw Sir Thomas' boat head out toward the anchor cables and the others continue on their way toward him to board. The *Hornet* was moving slowly through the water as the men heaved on the capstan bars. She would touch bottom every now and then but only gently. If he could get as much as three inches more clearance under his keel, he could sail out. But he had lightened the brig as much as he could without parting with his guns. For a moment he wondered whether he should not have tumbled his guns over earlier. It was too late to attempt it now. Forty of his crew were over the side in boats and were unarmed. He hoped Lears and Clemens had enough sense to fend for themselves. The British boats were only four hundred yards away, and what had to be done must be done in a hurry.

"Strike out the reef in the topgallants and set fore- and mainstaysails," he shouted to Hawkins and went back to take the helm. The operation would take five minutes if nothing went wrong. By that time the British boats would be down upon him and his cables would be cut. The sails were set one by one. Hawkins himself went aloft to help shake the reefs out of the topgallants, his long thin legs straddling the yard and his coattails flying over his head in the wind.

The sails had to be slacked off to untie the reef points, and started to hammer in the wind, shaking the yards on which the men were perched. But the men were used to their work, and soon the topgallants, much enlarged in area now, were trimmed, and the *Hornet*, under the increased weight of canvas, heeled over slightly in the water.

The staysails were already on their stays, lashed with marlin against the masts. One man could free each sail which could then be hauled up on its halyard from the deck. But the men seemed disastrously slow.

Ahead, Sir Thomas' boat had now reached the anchor cable, and a seaman was hacking at it with a cutlass. He had a difficult job of it, for the cable kept rising and falling in the water with the tossing of the brig.

The four British boats were almost under the bowsprit. The men from the *Hornet*'s two boats were swarming aboard, not wanting to face the British boat crews without arms.

Hawkins was down from the tops and without consulting Peace of God had Simmons, the master gunner, issue cutlasses and boarding pikes to the crew. But at the capstans the men were still hauling in on the anchors.

Suddenly the cable to one of the anchors was severed. The shock shook the brig like a blow, and her head veered away for a second. Four or five of the British boarding party had gained the bowsprit from one of the boats, climbing up the dolphin striker. Three were shaken off into the water as the brig staggered under the release of the cable. Another of the British boats had got a grappling hook over the larboard rail, and her men were swarming up onto the deck using the foremast chain plates.

A brisk fight was developing there. Peace of God saw and sensed these things but could not concentrate on them. The safety of the brig was now in his hands alone. What he did in the next sixty or seventy seconds would decide the day.

With more sail on her she was heeling over in the water. That was what he needed. Heeled over, even with her rounded sides, she would draw four or five inches less water. But he was still held by the last cable, and the men, heaving on the capstan, were hauling her up into the wind. If her yards were taken aback, she would come to a stop in the water and, when the cable was cut, drive backwards on the sands which were but fifty feet off.

Hawkins saw the danger. He had come aft despite the fight at the foremast chain plates, because he sensed that he now must take fighting command of the ship. He shouted something to Peace of God, seized an ax and with two strokes severed the last anchor cable.

For a moment the *Hornet*, released of her last hold on the bottom, flung wildly aside. Then, caught in some swirl of the tide, she swung around until her topgallants were flapping as they lost the wind and she came upright in the water. There was a scraping sound from her hull, felt rather than heard through the deck. Peace of God spun the wheel through his hands to leeward, staring at the flapping topgallants. Slowly the *Hornet's* head fell downwind. Then, in a fraction of a second and with a report like cannon shot, the topgallants filled, the brig heeled over and, hesitating for but a moment, pushed her blunt nose through the water, piling the dirty foam around her forefoot.

There was a second now to look around. The British

boarders, feeling the ship get under way, were throwing themselves over the side. Peace of God caught a glimpse of Sir Thomas Greenhow in his boat no more than fifty yards away. He was waving his arms, signaling for his boats to give chase. There was still the chance that the *Hornet* might strike another sand bar, for she was not yet in the channel, though certainly over the divide of the sands. He could see the channel off to windward—an area of comparatively quiet water, much darker than the gray and white cauldron through which he was now plunging.

Then the *Hornet* struck again. The impact knocked Peace of God against the wheel, and every man on deck was hurled from his feet. A rack containing cannon shot burst, and the balls rolled with a grumbling, thundering sound over the deck planks. There was a cheer from the British boats, heard only faintly above the roar of the tide and the wind. The brig was only just aground. She moved an inch or two and then stopped and then moved an inch more. Caught on the bottom, with her sails set, she slewed around, turning her stern toward the gale.

Again it was Hawkins who saved the situation. "Hands to sheets and braces," he shouted. "Trim all home taut and stand by."

The sails pulled flat against the wind now tilted the brig over heavily, and she inched forward, scraping her bottom on the sand but still moving. And then in one joyous triumphant moment she came free.

"Close haul and sheet fast," roared Hawkins. Peace

of God spun the helm to windward, and the *Hornet* headed once more for the channel.

She made the channel without further grounding, leaving the British boats astern. But to sail down the channel the brig would have to cross the wind.

"Stand by to go about," shouted Hawkins, and the men tailed on to the sheets and braces.

"Ready about," cried Peace of God. He brought the brig off the wind for a moment, to give her more speed through the water, and then spun the wheel hard to windward. Round she came, her yards backing for a moment as they crossed the wind, and then filling again. Peace of God held her off the wind for a while until she had regained speed and then brought her close to it, the men trimming sheets and braces.

He had to repeat the maneuver once more when they came to a bend in the channel. The channel followed close inshore of the northeast extremity of the island of Texel and it was there that he had to go about again.

The maneuver was done without difficulty, though the brig had to come so close to the island that a man aboard the *Hornet* could have tossed a marlinespike onto the beach. There were several of the islanders on the beach. They had come to see the fun and they cheered as the brig veered off and headed out to the open sea, and several of them shouted something and pointed seaward across the headland. Their words were lost in the screaming of the wind which, now that they were headed to open water, increased its violence.

Once they cleared the headland, the men on the *Hor-*

net discovered what the islanders were trying to tell them. Four miles to windward and scudding along under her topsails was the frigate *Cerebus,* coming down toward them. She was between them and the open sea and could cut them off. And if they got within range of her guns, the *Cerebus* could blow the *Hornet* to matchwood with half a broadside.

"Break out the Union Jack over the Continental colors, Mr. Hawkins," said Peace of God. For a moment, Hawkins hesitated, not seeming to understand the order.

Then he gave the vestige of a smile, and the British colors were run up to fly over those of the Continental Congress.

This was the procedure when a prize was taken—to fly the captor's colors over those of the vanquished. The officers on the *Cerebus,* seeing them run up, and knowing their captain had himself led the boat party in after the *Hornet,* would presume that he had taken her and was coming out to rejoin the frigate on the captured brig.

For a few minutes the *Cerebus* continued on her course. The distance between them was but a matter of two miles—well within cannon shot. Then the *Cerebus* turned into the wind, backing her main yards to remain heaved-to until the *Hornet* was brought alongside her, so that Sir Thomas Greenhow could triumphantly board his own ship.

Peace of God altered his course to come a little closer to the *Cerebus* and allay suspicions. He realized that he had too many men on deck. As a prize there would be only a small crew aboard, his own crew being confined to the forecastle below decks.

"All hands below except the deck watch," he ordered, and all the men scuttled for the forecastle hatch and tumbled down the ladder. He eyed the *Cerebus* through the murk, thinking over the problem that confronted her officer.

It was a habit of his, whenever he saw a vessel at sea, to analyze the problems of the man in command, and this habit stood him in good stead now. The tide was running fast and into the teeth of the wind. The officer on the *Cerebus*, by backing his main yards, could hope to keep the frigate headed into the wind, but the tide would keep trying to slew her stern around. She would be hard to handle in those conditions and the sensible thing to do would be to come to anchor.

This was particularly true if another vessel was going to come alongside, or the two might collide.

Hoping to encourage the officer in charge of the *Cerebus*, he now altered course more surely toward her. And then he had his reward. There was a little splash from the bow of the frigate as her anchor went down. He kept on his course until he was sure that the anchor was on the bottom and the frigate riding on it. It would take ten minutes to get the anchor up and ten more to get the frigate under sail again. Twenty minutes then. In twenty minutes he could be three, maybe three and a half miles away.

"Square away the yards, Mr. Hawkins," he shouted, "and get the fore- and mainsails on her. Tumble up all hands."

He put the helm over to bring the brig with the wind on her larboard beam, and soon she was flying through the North Sea, away from the frigate with the water washing over her lee rail. There was a report from the *Cerebus*, and a shot whipped through the air and plunged into the sea two hundred yards astern of the *Hornet*.

"Course north by east," said Peace of God to the helmsman who was standing by him, and turned over the wheel to him. He then went aft to his cabin.

He was dead tired. He had no feeling in his hands or below his knees and on his way back to his tiny cabin he started to shiver violently. He threw himself down on his bunk in his soaking clothing and reached up and got a book down from a shelf over his head. Its title was *Appeals to Men of Reason and Religion* by John Wesley. But he had hardly opened it before he fell asleep.

9

Three weeks later every port in England was astir with news of the American raider which had been operating in both the Channel and the North Sea and which, in that time, had sunk or taken as prizes twenty thousand tons of merchant shipping. The first victim was the snow *Christine*, rounding the North Foreland at the end of the Channel narrows, with a cargo of Manchester woolen goods.

She had been brought to with a single salvo, boarded almost within sight of land, and taken to Dunkirk in France as a prize. Then came the collier *Mary Bead* with nearly a thousand tons of coal aboard, taken off Flamborough Head and herded through the Straits of Dover in broad daylight to be handed over to prize agents in Le Havre. Then the West Indiaman *Tricolee*, sunk by gunfire with fifty thousand pounds' worth of rum and spices aboard in St. George's Channel. She was sunk, her master said, because the damned rascal of a Yankee captain hadn't enough of a prize crew to put aboard her and take her to France.

"By thunder," roared this individual, at a meeting of insurance subscribers in Lloyds, "it's a hard thing to bring a ship through a West Indian hurricane and a full gale off the Newfoundland banks, and then have her sunk—sunk, gentlemen—within one day's sail of Bristol."

The subscribers, who would have to reimburse the owners under the rules of Lloyds Insurance Agency, for the loss of ship and cargo, wanted more information. Had he fought this ship, they asked? He mounted six eight-pounders and the American brig had about the same. Had he fought at all or had he struck in sheer terror?

"I fought," roared the captain. "With my shot flying high over the Yankee's topmasts and every round of his thumping into my hull at the water line. Eight-pounders, you say, and you ask what could an eight-pounder do to a West Indiaman planked with eight-inch oak? Well, gentlemen, this Yankee has some special way to use his guns. For every round of his hit within a yard of the other, and stove in my planks as if he had a thirty-two up against my hull. Five rounds and I was holed so bad I had a fifteen-degree list to starboard and my guns useless, one side pointing up to the skies and the other down into the sea.

"Then, by God, this Yankee hails me and calls me a poor sinner like himself and says to get my men in the boats and trust in the mercy of the Lord who would support them, says he, on the great and roaring bosom of the ocean.

" 'What about my perishing cargo, you bloody-minded pirate?' I roared. 'Seven hundred hogshead of prime West Indian rum.'

" ' 'Tis the devil's brew, brother,' he cried. 'And 'twill kill fishes. Now if it will kill fishes, what will it do to men?' And with that he hauls his wind and heads north and all I hear is some kind of a hymn being sung by the men that weren't busy handling sails.

"Poor sinner," snorted the captain of the West India-man. "There'll be repentance enough in him when he's swinging from a gallows over the mud flats at Tilbury with the sea gulls fighting for the daintier bits of him."

"We must catch him first," said one of the subscribers. "That's the rummest go I've ever come across—a praying pirate. Though I've heard that Kidd was a great man at his prayers and gave a sermon before he was hung that brought tears from the eyes of two bishops."

The sinking of the *Tricolee* had been followed by the taking of two small coastal vessels, also sent as prizes into Le Havre, and the news of these raids had reached, it was rumored, to the thrones of France and England.

In England George III flew into such a violent rage that he had to be bled for twenty minutes to reduce his heat. In France Louis XVI nodded sagely on hearing the news and then turned to the task of setting the spring in a new lock which he had designed. Lockmaking was his hobby and it was said that he spent more time with his locksmith than with Necker, his chief minister.

At his country home in Passy, outside Paris, Dr. Benjamin Franklin was the only man in France who had the fullest details of the activities of Peace of God Manly, the sea captain from Salem who had stirred up so much trouble, and he had made excellent use of the news.

A word dropped here and there at entertainments among his fashionable neighbors—in the salon of pretty Madame Brillon whose husband worked in the French treasury, and the drawing room of Madame Helvetius, the respected widow of a famous philosopher—had produced a thousand rumors of the prowess of the Yankee captain with the strange name of Peace of God.

And indeed, in court circles in Paris it was held that Peace of God Manly had taken or sunk a score of British merchantmen, raided the naval dockyard at Portsmouth and bid defiance to two British ships of the line.

Monsieur de Vercennes, the French foreign minister, seeking to get to the bottom of these rumors, now called on Dr. Franklin, who received him in his study, and the two, as was their custom, seated themselves before a chessboard.

"This Peace of God Manly," said the Count de Vercennes, moving the king's pawn two spaces to open the game, "is undoubtedly far more formidable ashore than he is at sea."

"I'm not sure that I understand your meaning," replied Dr. Franklin, putting the queen's knight into play.

"Well, his victories as reported in the drawing rooms are undoubtedly far in excess of his victories on the narrow seas," replied Vercennes.

"Without a doubt," replied Dr. Franklin. "You know me as an honest man and I am not, in my declining years, going to try to deceive you. The total number of vessels taken or sunk by the *Hornet*, according to my last information, was six, and the tonnage twenty thousand. Her captain is reported in Paris to have taken a score of ships amounting to a tonnage five times in excess of the actual figure.

"But those victories are to be credited to me, since it is I who have encouraged belief in them. I only hope that Captain Manly will forgive me the deception and not think that I peril my soul in the cause of my country."

"I cannot understand why you spread these rumors," said Vercennes. "It is childish to spread reports of victories that do not exist."

"Not at all," said Dr. Franklin eying the chessboard and then moving his queen out boldly. "What is thought to be the truth is often more powerful than the truth itself. Therefore victories that are thought to have been won are often more important in their effect than victories that have actually been won.

"In the case of Peace of God Manly, by encouraging the belief of far more successes than he has attained, I stir up popular support for our cause. I create the impression that we are invincible—as indeed I think history will show that we are, in the present case.

"And these rumors, picked up by British intelligence agents and reported in England, spread dismay among the enemy, bring about a rise in marine insurance costs, bring demands on the Admiralty for more frigates to seek out the raider, bring demands that a convoy system be organized even in British waters, and may even result in British ships of war being withdrawn from our coast in America to protect British ports.

"All that is well worth a little deception."

"And yet," said the Count de Vercennes, taking Franklin's queen with his knight, "the British are a hardheaded and practical people. They will, after a while, reflect that it is only one small brig that is causing all this trouble. They will console themselves that the brig must inevitably be captured or sunk. And so there is no reason for them to panic."

"They are, as you say, a practical people," said Dr. Franklin advancing a pawn. "They are accustomed to deal in facts and figures and some of them are now reflecting on the high cost of killing Yankees. Here is the kind of arithmetic some of them are doing at the present time. Up to the battle of Bunker Hill, their expenses in the war were three million pounds. At that time they had killed about a hundred and fifty Americans. This cost them twenty thousand pounds per man killed. In the meantime, I would venture that sixty thousand more children have been born in America. So all is a dead loss.

"Now, in the matter of the brig *Hornet*. The total prizes she has taken or sunk amount to one hundred thousand pounds of cargo and perhaps the same again in ships. That is two hundred thousand pounds direct loss. To that can be properly added the expenses of the several ships which are now in search of the *Hornet*. Let us put that at five hundred pounds a week. All this, because of one American brig. Now if there were two of these, the expense might be doubled, and between the land war in America and the sea war around the British Isles, it is possible that some in England may be asking themselves whether the nation is to be bankrupt before achieving victory."

"You do not impress me, my dear doctor," said Vercennes. "It is only one brig and will soon be captured."

Dr. Franklin reached out a puffy, old man's hand and moved a pawn.

"And this is only one pawn, my dear Count," he said. "And yet it has your king in check. Indeed, checkmate. You have busied yourself with your queen and your knights. But I have concerned myself with my little pawns and won the game."

"War is not a game of chess," said Vercennes.

"You are mistaken there," replied Dr. Franklin. "More and more it becomes a game of chess. You see America as a nation with no queens or bishops or knights—only pawns. Yet pawns are powerful when fighting for their lives—pawns, like our farmers at Bunker Hill and our frontiersmen at Saratoga and this humble fisherman from Salem out on the winter's sea with his brig, the *Hornet*, challenging the British Navy in their home waters. There is a lot of strength in pawns and in a nation built of pawns—or peasants as you call them here in France."

"What kind of a man is this Peace of God Manly?" asked the Count. "Everybody is talking of him here in Paris. Is it possible to meet him?"

"He is a man of religion," replied Franklin, "which means a man of duty. He is a humble man, but a staunch one."

"I am curious about him," said Vercennes. "He will of course be an ambitious man and expect great rewards for what he has done."

"He wants only to return to his cottage in Salem and to his daughter Nancy."

"Nothing more?"

"Nothing more."

"But surely there is something he must seek as a reward for his valor."

Dr. Franklin was rearranging the chessmen on the board, and seemed for a while lost in thought. When he had all the pieces in place he looked at them carefully and then said, "Before he went on his present cruise, he wrote a letter to his daughter which I read, for it is my business to do such things. In it he expressed the hope that he would be able to bring her a length of blue ribbon for her use. It seems that it is something she has long desired."

"How charming," said Vercennes. "How completely charming. But of course it is only a matter of time before he will be taken. There are enough spies among the fishermen to pass on word of his whereabouts. And then he will either be killed in action or taken prisoner and hung and there will be no ribbon for his daughter Nancy."

"That may be his fortune," said Dr. Franklin heavily. "And I assure you from the bottom of my heart that of all the men whose lives I must commit to jeopardy in the course of this war, I wish this man Peace of God safe at home."

"Why him in particular?" asked Vercennes. And then with a slight smile he said, "You will forgive my suggesting it, but is there perhaps some connection with the daughter Nancy? You are quite a charmer among the ladies here in France, my dear doctor."

"I am old enough to be their grandfather," said Dr. Franklin, "and so have liberty to use whatever charm I possess on them without hurt to their pretty hearts or heads. But there is about this man, Peace of God, a sort of essence of my own country and its people. He has come to stand for me as a symbol for them all. And so I heartily wish him safe, and yet must expose him to peril."

"Well, as I have said before," said the count, "he will undoubtedly be taken, and that soon."

"I do not agree with you, for this man has the same motto in the face of hazard as that which I propose we should adopt for our nation," replied Dr. Franklin.

"And what motto is that?" asked the count.

"In God We Trust, sir," said Dr. Franklin. "In God We Trust."

Meanwhile, a man whose idle moments seemed spent in cutting patterns out of pieces of papers with a pair of scissors presented himself at Lloyds of London in their new offices at the Royal Exchange and asked for an interview with the chief subscribers who had sustained so heavy a loss on the sinking of the West Indiaman *Tricolee*.

He gave his name as Sir Benjamin Meadows, and since his clothes were of the best quality and his manner authoritative and his accents refined, he was taken to a waiting room and there provided with a dish of coffee—this being the old custom at Lloyds.

After a little while another clerk, of higher station, came to inquire what might be the gentleman's business, to which he had replied, "Money. I have need of a large amount, for my expenses are rather high."

This had completely baffled the clerk who spoke to one of the subscribers and persuaded him to see the gentleman who called himself Sir Benjamin Meadows.

With this individual, Sir Benjamin was a little more open. He said he was acquainted with the captain of the American brig, *Hornet*, and had a plan for the capture of the brig in which the subscribers would be interested, in view of their heavy insurance losses. But he declined to discuss the matter further, saying he would lay the full details of his plan only before a meeting of the whole membership.

The meeting was agreed for the following day. Sir Benjamin, excellently dressed, and wearing a handsome pair of white silk hose (which in truth was the last pair at his disposal) attended the meeting, carrying a chart of the waters around the British Isles. On this he had noted the exact places at which the *Hornet* had taken or sunk prizes. This then gave the route of the *Hornet* since leaving Texel. One of the subscribers, looking over the chart, complained that there was nothing there they did not know already.

"We know the *Hornet* is somewhere in the Irish Sea," he growled. "You are wasting your time, sir, giving us information of which both we and the Admiralty are already in possession."

"If you do not wish to hear any more, gentlemen," said Sir Benjamin, reaching for his chart, "I assure you I have other business to attend to."

"Hoity-toity, man," said one of the subscribers. "Don't be so quick to take offense. If you have something to tell us of value, be sure that we will listen and gladly pay for the information. But first of all I should like to know something about yourself. If, for instance, you have more exact knowledge of the whereabouts of the *Hornet*, why have you not taken it to the Admiralty?"

"The Admiralty?" said Sir Benjamin coolly. "Why should I take my information to the Admiralty? Surely you gentlemen are aware of the fact that the First Lord of the Admiralty is concerned only with knowing whether his opponent holds the ace of spades when he has only the king. Beyond gambling he has no other interest." There was a chuckle at the thrust.

"Well, sir," said one of the subscribers. "You say you know where the *Hornet* is? Where is she?"

Sir Benjamin leaned with his arms on the table and

put his face so close to the man who spoke that their noses almost touched. "What will you pay?" he asked.

The man addressed looked uncertainly about at his fellows and then said, "For sure information, five thousand pounds." The rest grunted their approval.

"And for her capture—or destruction?" asked Sir Benjamin.

"Ten thousand."

Sir Benjamin shook his head. "Make it twenty thousand, gentlemen," he said.

There was a rumble of dissent.

"Come, sirs," said Sir Benjamin. "The loss of the *Tricolee* cost you upwards of thirty thousand pounds. There are four West Indiamen on their way in from Jamaica now—the *Trident, Godspeed, Spica,* and *William Hope.* They left Jamaica seven weeks ago. They are nearing the Irish coast at this moment—somewhat dispersed as a result of heavy weather, I might add. You gentlemen have insured them all—ships and cargo. Would it not be wise in these days to take out a little more insurance—twenty thousand pounds' worth—to make certain these ships reach Bristol?"

"Where do you get this information from?" someone asked.

"That is my concern," said Sir Benjamin. "What concerns you is whether it is accurate information. For therein lies a test of the efficiency of my intelligence." The subscribers looked at each other and nodded. The information was accurate. The four West Indiamen had been reported by a fast packet as approaching the coast of Ireland and dispersed due to gales.

"Before we agree to your price, tell us something of your plan for taking the *Hornet*," said one of the sub-scribers.

"I will tell you nothing of it," said Sir Benjamin, "for in these matters there is always too much chatter. But I can give you this much without danger. Peace of God Manly before he took to—er—piracy—was a fisherman. As such he has a great regard for fishermen of all nationalities."

"From this may we assume that some kind of fishing vessel will be used in the plot?" asked someone.

"You may assume what you wish," replied Sir Benjamin. "My terms are simple. You will agree to pay me, as of this moment, five thousand pounds. You will deposit a further fifteen thousand pounds in a bank of my choice in my name with the proviso that it is not to be handed to me until you have proof of the destruction or capture of the brig *Hornet*."

"What security have we got that if we advance you five thousand pounds as of this moment that you will not walk away with it and we shall not see you again?"

"None whatever," said Sir Benjamin cheerfully. "And in return may I ask what security you have got that your four West Indiamen are going to reach Bristol safely? A nice prize there, gentlemen. Particularly since the *William Hope* is leaking and her hands are engaged, watch in and watch out, working her pumps to keep her afloat. She lags behind the others and should be easy to pick off for a man with the audacity of our Yankee pirate."

"We have asked the Admiralty to send a frigate to her

assistance," said one of the subscribers, blushing with irritation that so much of his affairs should be known to the cool gentleman before them.

"Your request was forwarded to the Earl of Sandwich at his own house," said Sir Benjamin. "But he had left for Brighton with His Royal Highness the Prince Regent where I believe a boxing match has been arranged on which the earl has wagered two thousand pounds. Gentlemen John Jackson against Lancashire Jeremy. I should hazard it will be three days before his lordship received your request and a week, I fancy, before the frigate is dispatched. Which would, of course, be much too late."

There was a conference of looks among the subscribers and then their spokesman nodded. "You shall have five thousand pounds within the hour," he said, "and the rest will be deposited as you propose."

"Thank you, gentlemen," said Sir Benjamin. "It is always a pleasure to do business with men of sense. Anticipating your agreement, I had already made my plans." He summoned them around the chart, pointing to an area off the Head of Kinsale off the Irish coast.

10

For two days the *Hornet* had been fighting her way out
of the Channel in storm winds which had worked stead-
ily from the north to the west, until they were now
due west. Her crew was much reduced. Clemens and
Lears, her second and third officers, had gone back to
Le Havre with prizes, leaving Peace of God with only
one officer, the taciturn Hawkins. Between them, the
two officers had taken thirty crewmen, so that aboard
the brig there were now but thirty left and these much
worn with the labor of working the ship in such vile
weather.

The weather had indeed hardly improved since the escape from Texel. There had been snow and sleet and hail and seas shipped green over the *Hornet*'s sturdy bow. The forecastle had had to be pumped out twice. The men's bedding was wet with no prospect of it being dried in the near future, and most of them were suffering from salt-water sores.

Simmons, the master gunner, was in a particularly poor state. Not only had he sores on his wrists and ankles (the usual locations due to the chafing of cuffs on the skin) but his face had broken out in a mass of carbuncles so that he looked as if he had been stung by a great number of bees. It was no small part of Peace of God's troubles that he was unable to keep his master gunner sober whenever there was any leave in France. The brig had touched at Dunkirk and at Le Havre after leaving Texel, and on each occasion Simmons had managed to drink himself insensible. It was a puzzle where he got money with which to buy liquor, but Hawkins had said, "When it comes to grog, a seaman can always raise a shilling." Anyway, Simmons was all but useless and had taken to doctoring his carbuncles with a mixture of weevily flour and gunpowder, which he spread over his glowing and painful features.

Peace of God would not be taking the *Hornet* out of the channel but for intelligence he had received in Le Havre that four West Indiamen were on their way in, straggling apart from each other and much worn by the weather. He should have stayed in Le Havre to refit and collect the rest of his crew who had not arrived when he reached the French port. But he had been urged to get to sea immediately when there was a chance of picking off one of the West Indiamen when she rounded the Kerry heads on the Irish coast. Duty compelled him to undertake the venture which his sense of seamanship told him was rash.

Foul weather, then, and half a crew and most of these crippled with sores. It was a poor condition in which to undertake a venture which should be tackled only with his ship and crew in top condition.

All morning, after clearing the Scillies off the coast of Cornwall, there had been a driving rattle of hail flinging out of leaden skies. It drove down so thick that the wild Channel water seemed to be peppered with musket shot. This turned by midmorning to a thin hard sleet, so thick that it was impossible to see from one end of the ship to the other. Then, as the temperature rose, came rain and finally by noon the weather had cleared, though the wind still piped strong out of the west. Bellying dark clouds were pressed down upon the ocean so that near the horizon sea and clouds seemed united. But visibility had increased to a mile and there was in this something for which to be thankful.

In his cabin Peace of God now found time to look over the men on his sick list. He had a rough medical knowledge and although on most vessels of this size it was the practice for the crew to doctor each other, except in grave cases, it was his habit to look over his men himself daily. This gave him a chance of doctoring not only their bodies but their souls. It also kept him intimately in touch with the over-all condition of his hands.

Dickie, the powder boy, was first on the list. His thin

wrists were a raw mass of salt-water sores, and the pain from these was so intense that he shivered as if from the ague, and his face was white and hot.

"What brought you to sea, lad?" Peace of God asked, gently rolling up the sleeve of the boy's sea coat so as not to hurt him too greatly.

"Farming, sir," said the boy, staring at the mass of suppurating red sores on his wrist and arms. "I was tired of horses and plows and milking and drawing water and cutting wood and the like. I'd heard of them islands with palm trees and the sun always strong and the sea, they said, as blue as a marebell. My brother, he went into the army. But it was the West Indian island I couldn't get out of my head with the coconuts in the trees and apes, they do say, that will throw them down to you if you have any luck."

"You ran away, then," said Peace of God sternly. "And what of your parents at home, fretting to know where you are?"

"I didn't think of that, sir, until I'd signed on. But 'tis done now. And when I get back I'll stay with them and never roam again."

Peace of God shook his head. "Thou wilt not, Dickie," he said. "Thou'll be ashore perhaps two weeks and then away to sea again. The sea is like strong drink that once you have tasted you can never give it up. Are your bowels working regular?"

"Yes, sir," said Dickie and he was young enough to blush.

"If they don't, come to me and I'll give you a draft of pitch water. There is no cure for these sores but to keep them dry and get the sun on them and that cannot be done in this weather. But there's something will take the pain from them." He unscrewed the container of the lantern in his cabin, took a length of rag and poured some of the whale oil from the lantern on the rag. When it was soaked he wrapped the rag around the boy's arm and did the same with the other.

"Do they hurt less now, lad?"

"Yes, sir," said the boy.

"Tomorrow take off these rags, wash your arms in fresh water and come aft again and I will bandage them once more. Do you say your prayers, boy?"

"No, sir. Only when I'm afraid down there in the powder hold and the ship in action."

"To pray to be saved in danger is well enough," said Peace of God. "But you should pray also in gratitude for your creation so that you may be saved when you die and join the glorious hosts around the throne of God. All here is but preparation for that eternity of joy or of damnation. I have something for you will give you more rest than all the whale oil I put on your sores." He reached under his bunk, pulled out his sea chest, opened it, and produced a printed sheet with the title "Thoughts from the Sermons of John Wesley."

"Read that and ponder on it," said Peace of God, "and you will welcome the fiery pain in your arms as a means of salvation." The boy looked disappointed, and so Peace of God, rummaging in his sea chest, found a tin box and, opening it, took out a small sugar cake.

"Take this also," he said. " 'Twas made by my daughter Nancy. You may have another tomorrow."

The next on the sick list was Simmons, and with him Peace of God was far from gentle. The master gunner's face was distorted by the carbuncles on it which puffed his cheeks to such an extent that his mouth was twisted out of shape.

"Well, Mr. Simmons," said Peace of God, "I see the hand of Satan on you. The drink he has put in your mouth with promises of ease and cease of care has burst out on your face now like hot coals from the pit of hell. And bad as your body looks, it is but an imperfect mirror of the condition of your soul, which is seeping with the sores of sinful living."

"Amen to that, sir," said Simmons. "That's more truth than poetry, as the Good Book tells us."

"There is no such saying in the Good Book, Master Simmons," said Peace of God. "How are your bowels?"

"Poorly, sir," said the gunner. "Not what I'd call ship-shape."

"We must purge you of evil, then. Drink all of this. It is bitter like the waters of salvation which do not go down like milk but gripe at the throat and retch the stomach and yet must be swallowed if we are to be saved." He produced a pannikin of water from which came a mixed aroma of pitch and sulphur so strong that Simmons half turned his face away when the pannikin was put in his hands.

"Ah, Mr. Simmons," said Peace of God. "The purge is hard to take, so you turn your face away from it. Poor miserable soul. Why cannot you turn away your face from the rum that brings on the boils that make the purge necessary? The devil has you in his snare, Master Gunner. He makes that which is evil for you taste sweet and that which is good for you taste foul. So sinning is pleasant for you, and prayer and mortification by which alone you can be saved, comes hard. But I am determined that you shall have two medicines at one time, for I am your captain, Master Gunner, and your safety, body and soul, is committed to my hands. Drink up the purge."

With enormous distaste the master gunner raised the pannikin to his lips and started to drink. He would have stopped after a swallow or two, but Peace of God reached out and held the pannikin up against Simmons' mouth, at the same time tilting his head back so that he must either drink it or drown in it.

"And now," said Peace of God, "let us go down on our knees together like brothers and pray God to save us from the wiles of Satan. Let us call upon him in a loud voice like the psalmist, and he will hear us even from the depths of our iniquity."

The master gunner had no more stomach for praying than he had for drinking the purge of sulphur water and pitch. But down on his knees he went, with Peace of God beside him, and they were in this position when Hawkins, after a perfunctory knock, opened the cabin door to stare at them in astonishment for a moment.

"There is a small vessel off our starboard bow, down by the head, and seems sinking," he said, staring wooden-faced at Peace of God who was still upon his knees.

"Can you make anything of her?" asked Peace of God, looking up from the prayer book he held open in his rough hands.

"Bristol built lugger, I'd say," replied Lieutenant Hawkins. "Fisherman."

At the word Peace of God rose, and the gunner got up also, rather faster, and pushing his way from the cabin, staggered to the rail where he leaned for a while, retching.

Peace of God went on deck and, climbing into the mainmast shrouds, peered into the scud. For a while he could see nothing but the big green-backed waves, their tops roaring white, which heaved in out of the Atlantic. Then he glimpsed the vessel for a moment, raised on the back of one of these rollers. She seemed down by the head and her foremast gaff was cockabill—the end allowed to drop down, which was a signal of distress. The waves seemed to be breaking over her foredeck.

"She's sinking," said Peace of God.

"What's she doing out in this weather anyway?" demanded Hawkins.

"Caught by the storm, taking in her nets," replied the captain.

"This storm has been blowing two weeks," said Hawkins. "There's been no fishing in these waters all that while. The fishing fleets are all in port."

"What do you think then?" asked Peace of God.

Hawkins had been examining the stricken lugger through a telescope. He snapped it shut and said, "I don't like it. We are not ten miles off the head of Kinsale. She could have run there for shelter and made it in three hours. Why stand to a sea anchor waiting for help to come?"

But Peace of God had already made up his mind. "Gun crews to their stations," he said, and gave the helmsman a new course which would take the *Hornet* to the lugger. They were upon her in forty minutes, and coming up to windward, her captain hailed the *Hornet*.

"Sinking fast," he shouted. "Two planks stove and three men hurt. Can you take me in tow to Kinsale?"

"I cannot," shouted Peace of God, "and thou art no seaman to ask, for towing will sink her the faster. How did you stave in her planks?"

"Trawl cables broke," was the reply. "I've three men hurt below. If you won't tow me, can you take us off?"

"I don't like it," said Hawkins. "Only a fool would have his trawl down in weather like this."

"Lower away a boat," said Peace of God. He caught sight of Simmons standing beside one of the guns and said, "Join the boat's crew, Mr. Simmons. Work will purge thee the better."

"Aye, aye, sir," said the master gunner, who, whatever his faults, had no pity for himself. Dickie jumped into the boat, too, though unbidden.

The two vessels were but sixty feet apart, the *Hornet* hove to but creeping forward of the lugger which was drifting astern on a sea anchor. By the time the boat was in the water, the *Hornet* was up off the lugger's bow, which would be an advantage, for the boat would drift with wind and water down to the lugger, saving her crew the necessity of rowing. Simmons had taken charge of the boat and fastened her painter to the main halyard so that those aboard the *Hornet* could haul her back, and there would be no need for using oars. Simmons was a resourceful man, Peace of God noted, and not for the first time.

Hawkins was prepared to enter the boat when Peace of God stopped him. "I'll go," he said. "If there's men hurt aboard, I have a little skill in handling them." He jumped into the boat and with Simmons paying out on the main halyard they were soon down on the stricken lugger.

Her bow was very low in the water and only her captain and one other man were on deck. There was a tarpaulin cover rigged before the foremast which Peace of God took as a shelter for the men working the pumps. But he could not hear the clanking of the pull rods of the pumps and as soon as he stepped on deck felt uneasy. Simmons was right behind him and, spotting the canvas, was reminded of something he had seen before. He eyed the canvas for a moment and then, seizing Peace of God by the shoulders, he heaved him bodily back into the boat, jumping on top of him.

The master gunner was on his feet in a second, hauling in as fast as he could on the main halyard. "Thirty-two-pounder!" he shouted to Peace of God. "Snugged down under that canvas."

The next moment there was a tremendous explosion from the lugger, and the concussion was so great that the *Hornet*'s boat, between the lugger and the brig, was nearly swamped. In the same moment the *Hornet* heaved up on her side as a thirty-two-pound shot plowed through her stern quarter, toppled the mainmast and flung splinters of wood three and four feet long through the air.

The boat, released from the brig (for the main halyard had been cut when the mast went), swirled down toward the lugger and, coming broadside to the waves, was all but swamped. But the men aboard had their oars out in a second and turned her head to the seas and stopped her foundering.

In the same instant the thirty-two-pounder aboard the lugger fired again. The range was no more than a hundred feet. Those on the boat were deafened by the explosion of the gun and so hardly heard the even greater detonation when the *Hornet*'s powder room blew up.

They saw the explosion, though—saw a sheet of yellow flame split the brig in two and saw also the whole of her foredeck rise up into the air and then come down in the water. In the next second there was not a trace of the brig to be seen, though the water around was littered with wreckage. One of the men on the boat slumped forward on his oar, his chest impaled by a three-foot splinter of wood from the brig. Simmons tumbled him into the bilge and, taking the man's oar, started pulling away from the lugger.

The lugger's decks were now swarming with men, and two boats were launched to cut off the escape of Peace of God and those with him. There were some shouted orders from the deck of the lugger, and the boats returned to her side. Then the lugger turned her bow slowly around in the water, for she had anchors out on her other side and could maneuver with these.

Her thirty-two-pounder now pointed directly at the boat on which were the only survivors of the *Hornet*. The intent was plain. If those aboard did not stop rowing, they would be blown out of the water.

The decision whether to surrender or not was Peace of God's and his alone. There were four men in the boat (one of them dying if not already dead in the scuppers) and himself. If they surrendered, they would live, though as prisoners. If not, they would almost certainly die. For a fraction of a second he hesitated and in that moment caught sight of the master gunner Simmons, with his face distorted with carbuncles and his arms a mass of sores. He was heaving on his oar with a will. That decided Peace of God. It was possible to learn lessons in courage from sinners as well as from saints.

He put the tiller over so that the boat drew slowly out of the line of fire of the thirty-two-pounder.

"Give way all," he shouted. "Heartily, now lads." The little boat rose to the crest of a sea, slewed over the top and had hardly begun her descent into the trough beyond when the thirty-two-pounder spoke again. The shot plunged into the face of the wave they had just cleared, ricocheted straight up in the air for a hundred feet and then plopped harmlessly into the ocean. It had been so near that Peace of God could hear the hiss of it through the air.

They still had a chance—a very slim chance—to escape the lugger.

11

The sound of a heavy gun firing somewhere out to sea had been plainly heard in the village of Kinsale and had sent some of the fishermen, despite the roaring wind, out to the headland to see if they could catch a glimpse of what was going on. There were two distinct detonations, though some said they had heard three, and the half dozen men who went out to the headland believed that there must be a naval engagement taking place of which they had heard only a small part. They were clad in rough trousers of homespun material and wore heavy knitted sweaters called bawneens. But none were shod, for shoes were a luxury and a fisherman was best in his barefeet anyway.

It was more than mere curiosity that brought the men out in the blinding wind. There was the possibility of wreckage. After a gale, they normally combed the coast for whatever flotsam they could find. But with what seemed to be a fight at sea going on, a ship might be driven up on the rocks. And what they could get of her cargo before the militia arrived they would keep. So it was best to be on the scene early.

Michael Reagan was the leader of the fishermen. He was a big gray-haired man missing two fingers of his left hand. He had not lost them by violence but had been born short two fingers and because of this handicap—a great handicap for anyone destined to work on the sea—he had developed his cunning and skill and endurance more than the others. They acknowledged him as the best in the village and looked to him for leadership. He had been twice to France in his hooker and four times to the Galician coast of Spain, and this in itself set him up above his fellows who in their traveling stayed in home waters.

There was nothing to be seen in the waste of green-gray water whipped by the wind and melting into an obscurity of fury a few hundred yards beyond the headland. The waves, flinging themselves upon the rocks at the foot of the headland, withdrew leaving a seething wake twenty feet long which was sucked up in the next wave to make the assault. The noise of the sea was fierce and thunderous, and the men settled down to watch in a little cave under the brow of the headland.

Here, though the wind boomed over the top and the water crashed and sucked below, there was a little oasis of quiet and they could hear each other talk.

"Do you think it might have been a distress signal we heard?" asked one of the men when they were squatted in the cave, their arms locked before their knees. Crouched in the cave in their dripping clothing and their long and uncared-for hair hanging like so much seaweed about their dank shoulders, they looked like half a dozen drowned men themselves. There was a look of cadavers in their thin faces and bony bare feet.

"It was not a distress signal," said Michael Reagan with calm authority. "It was a gun they call a thirty-two-pounder. I heard one fired when I was in Portsmouth in England three years ago. It is the same kind of a sound. I could not mistake it." He spoke in Gaelic, the common language in country parts of both Ireland and Scotland.

"It would be a big warship then," said one of the men.

"It might be," said Reagan. "And yet it is strange that we heard but two shots. When great warships are fighting, they fire all their guns together, and the sound of it would shake every cabin in the country. And yet there were but two shots."

"What do you make of it then?" he was asked.

"I cannot make anything of it," said Reagan. "The sea is full of mysteries. A man cannot in a moment explain everything he sees or hears upon the sea in a storm. But I am wondering whether it has anything to do with the lugger we saw earlier in the day coming up the coast.

She seemed to lie low by the head as if she were sinking and yet she was under sail."

"Would you say it was a French lugger or an English lugger?"

"It was an English lugger," said Reagan. "The French set the foremast well up forward and this one had the foremast about the shoulders of the vessel. And yet she was down by her head and if she was not sinking, there was some reason for that."

"Would you take a guess at the reason, just to pass the time?" asked another.

"I would," said Reagan. "And I would put two things together and see what comes of them. The first of these things is the lugger that was down by the head, and the second of them is that there was a thirty-two-pounder fired out on the ocean about where the lugger would be. And what I make of it is this: that the lugger had aboard her, up forward, a thirty-two-pounder gun. It would weigh the better part of two tons, if not more, and that would put her head down. She would be what the English call a gunboat, with a special platform built to take the gun."

"They are a terrible people, the English," said one of the fishermen. "Isn't it dangerous enough to be sailing on the water, with the wind as wild as a tinker's wife, and not be firing guns at other ships that are in the same kind of danger? It is nothing but flying in the face of Providence to fight at sea."

"You talk like a child," said Reagan contemptuously. "When there is fighting to be done, fighting being dangerous itself, does it matter where the fighting takes place? My grandmother, who was a seer, said that the day would come when people would be flying through the air and fighting each other, and so I believe it will."

"God forbid I should live to see it," said the other.

"Did any of you bring a scrap of tobacco with you?" asked Reagan. One of the men reached in his pocket, and Reagan, stretching out his hand for the tobacco, froze for a moment in that position.

"Did you not hear anything?" he demanded of the others.

"I think I heard a gull cry, but it was so slight that it was like the memory of it rather than the cry itself."

"Hush," said Reagan suddenly, and listened again. Then, without another word, he dashed out of the cave and up to the bluff of the headland and looked around. And then he saw, out in the swirl of the water, a swamped boat, tossed like a chip among the heaving waves.

"There's men on it," cried another of the fishermen. "But whether they are dead or alive I cannot say."

"They will not live in the surf," shouted Reagan. "God have mercy on them, they will be broken on the rocks." Nonetheless he ran, followed by the others, down a little goat path from the headland that led to a formidable tangle of rocks below. One of the men had brought a length of rope, and without a word Reagan stripped himself of his clothing and tied one end of the rope around his waist. The rain was still pelting down and the place where he stood was a smother of spray from the waves dashing against the rocks. But the man seemed impervious to the cold and stood watching the seas intently and out beyond the surf the little black dot of a boat that now appeared and now disappeared. It seemed to him that one man aboard was trying to row and if he could get the boat a little to the right, he would have a chance of coming into a small bay with shingle on it. Otherwise one of the combers must pick the boat up and dash it on the rocks and all aboard would be killed.

"I will go out and bring him in, God willing," said Reagan. "Pay out the rope behind me, and if I disappear and do not come up again, haul me back." He waited until a big wave had come roaring into the little beach on which they stood, the sides of the wave being knocked into a smother of foam as they ripped and roared into the rocks on the two sides of the bay.

When the wave had burst with a shattering thunder on the beach and the water began to rush seaward into the aftersuck, Reagan flung himself into the ocean and was taken out with the sea. Those ashore saw him lifted up to the top of a newly formed wave and disappear in it. This wave also rose and burst, and beyond they could see Reagan swimming strongly out toward the boat. Twice he was lost from view altogether, once for almost a minute, and the men ashore, thinking him drowned, were about to pull him in when he reappeared again. It seemed that no boat, let alone a man, could live in the turmoil of the sea. And yet the swimmer survived, though lifted on waves that were fifteen and twenty feet high. Several times it seemed that he was within a few yards of the boat, and then he would be flung away from it by the waves. But at last he got to it and went aboard like an eel, and the men on shore saw him for a moment standing naked up forward and untying the rope which they knew he would now make fast to the forward seat of the waterlogged boat.

They knew what to do. They dared not and indeed could not heave the boat in to land. But they must keep a strain on the rope, guiding the boat toward the little beach while the men aboard helped as much as they might by rowing her away from the rocks toward which she was being driven.

This seemed an impossible task. The seas, running back from the rocks, crashed into those being driven toward them by the wind and threw columns of water up in the air. Then for a moment there would be a curious quiet. And then another sea would gather for the assault. In this maelstrom the men on the boat worked to bring her around out of the maw of rocks and ocean. At first it had seemed to those ashore that there was only one man working at the oars in the boat. But they now made out that there were two—three including Reagan who had joined them at the oars.

Inch by inch they fought to get the boat away from the swirl of the seas by the rocks, at times gaining a foot, at others losing several feet, but always fighting. At one point the watchers saw the boat raised high on a wave so that it seemed to be above the level of their own heads.

"They're gone," cried one of the fishermen, but his words were lost in the wind. But the boat survived. It slipped out of the grip of the wave just as the wave broke and dashed itself against the rocks. For thirty seconds the boat was lost to sight. And then again it reappeared, this time a little closer to the beach.

The struggle went on for nearly half an hour. But finally the boat was brought opposite the beach, and the men ashore waited until they saw a big comber build up behind it. When the comber came, Reagan and the others aboard started rowing as fast as they could and, gaining some speed, the wave lifted the boat and came hissing ashore with it. The men on the beach dropped the rope, which was now useless, and waited. They saw the comber break, lost sight of the boat for an instant, and then saw it reappear. It was dashed up on the beach half under the water, and they seized it by the gunwales, and, themselves covered by the wave, hung on, holding their breath and digging their bare feet into the freezing pebbles which sucked and swirled around them so that they sank into the shingle to their knees.

But they did not let go of the boat. If they let go, the boat would be taken out in the aftersuck of the same wave which had brought it in, and it would be broken to pieces in the next wave. So they held on, and when the wave had receded, Reagan jumped from the boat and half dragged one of the men with him. The other fishermen helped, getting another big man by the armpits and hauling him from the boat.

There were two others, and some of the fishermen had got these halfway out of the boat when the next wave came and rescuer and rescued were bowled by the wave over and over, water and rocks storming around them, but holding fast the one to the other.

When the wave receded, the men were able to quickly drag the others to safety and they sat or lay in the howling of the wind and the beating of the rain and the spray, unable to do more than suck air into their lungs, their mouths open and hungry for air like so many suffocating fish.

After a little while Reagan got up slowly and the others followed him. He found his clothes and put on his trousers and they went with him to his cabin, which was apart from the others in the village and very close to the beach.

Reagan's wife, who had been standing in the stormy road with a shawl over her head waiting for news, saw the party of men coming and ran to her husband. He shouted something to her, and she went up the road in the direction of the nearest house. The men struggled up the little road, strewn with seaweed from the storm, and went into Reagan's cabin. Here the men from the boat were laid on the floor which was of hard packed clay.

There were three men taken from the boat and a boy. The face of one of the men was covered with boils. It was blue with cold and his lips were swollen. But he seemed the strongest of the survivors. The boy was unconscious, and Reagan felt his chest under his torn jersey and found a flicker of a heartbeat. He said something, and a fisherman brought a stone bottle out of which some liquid was poured and rubbed vigorously on the boy's wrists and ankles. The smell of this liquid immediately interested the man whose face was covered with boils, and he asked for some of it. But catching the eye of the third man, a small man of about sixty years of age, very tough-looking, the man with the boils on his face passed the stone bottle back with a sigh.

The fourth man was dead. He had not died of drowning but of some terrible wound that had been made in his chest.

Reagan turned to the older man who seemed as if he might be in charge and said in English, "What name do you have?"

"Peace of God Manly," said the other. "I am one of John Wesley's poor sinners."

"Were you sunk by the lugger?"

"I was," said Peace of God. "But the lugger was only the instrument the Lord chose to humble me for my pride. For I had become vain and took pride in my own achievements, forgetting that all things are done under the hand of God. And so he chastised me."

"What does he say?" asked one of the fishermen in Irish.

"It was the English lugger that sunk him but he thinks it was the hand of God," replied Reagan, with a trace of a smile.

"A man of his age should be able to tell the difference," said the other.

"Will you hush for a moment while I get some more out of him," said Reagan harshly. He turned again to Peace of God. "You'll be a Yankee, I'm thinking," said Reagan.

"I am from Salem, in Massachusetts," said Peace of God.

"I know you now," said Reagan. "There is a price on

your head. A hundred sovereigns. It is more money than you will find in Kinsale if you counted every copper that came into the village in five years."

The man with the boils on his face, hearing this, got up unsteadily to his feet. He had a sailor's knife in his belt and he pulled it out of the sheath. Reagan looked at him calmly.

"Look to your manners," he said mildly. "Do you think we are savages in this part of the world to bring drowning men into our houses and then sell them to our enemies? Besides, we have no love for the English here. You have your quarrel with them now, but ours is hundreds of years older. You are newcomers to the fight."

Having said this, Reagan looked at the dead man. "That one we will have to take down and throw in the sea again," he said. He nodded to two of the fishermen who started to pick up the body.

"He must be given a Christian burial," said Peace of God. "You cannot throw him back like a dog into the water."

"Put him down on the beach," said Reagan, "and tell the militia that there is a Yankee washed ashore and dead of wounds. We will have to hide the rest of you. If you are found in anyone's cabin, it will not only be your lives but ours as well. But we are old hands at hiding men in this part of the world."

"Couldn't you bury my mate decently?" asked the man with the boils, who was, of course, the gunner Simmons.

"If there was a fight at sea, the English will look for bodies washed ashore," said Reagan. "If they find one, they will think the rest of you were killed and the fish got you. But if they find none at all, they will be suspicious. Take him down to the beach. The other three of you will hide in the turf house. The militia will search the place, and after that we will see what is to be done."

Reagan's wife had by now returned with several other women so that the little cabin was crowded with people. The women managed to get the boy warm and after a while his heart beat more strongly and he recovered consciousness.

"God's curse on the man who lets go a single word about these men being here to any of the militia," said Reagan to the others.

"You should not call on God to curse your fellow men," said Peace of God. "It is a sacrilegious thing to do and will bring harm on you."

"You are a strange man," said Reagan. "I take you half drowned from the sea and you preach me a sermon."

"It is because I fear for your soul, brother, but I thank you for saving me also," said Peace of God.

12

Peace of God Manly with Simmons and the powder boy Dickie spent almost three weeks in the village of Kinsale, hidden in the turf house of Mike Reagan. In the meantime the militia three times visited the village and searched all the cottages.

The first time their visit was expected, for they had been sent for, and the body of the drowned seaman and the fragments of the boat were shown to the captain in charge. He seemed satisfied that there had been no other survivors.

But then a rumor reached him that three other men

had escaped and were hidden somewhere in Kinsale. And so he twice raided the village and ordered a search of all the cottages and the little houses, built for the most part of driftwood, in which each cottager kept his supply of turf for the winter.

On the last occasion the raid was made at three in the morning and the militia arrived a hundred strong. But the villagers of Kinsale were as crafty as foxes when it came to such raids, for they had hidden many a man with a price on his head. Reagan's turf house was floored with rough boards. Two of these, readily pulled aside, revealed below a tunnel down which the three seamen escaped, and going along the tunnel found themselves after a while in the little cave on the headland where Reagan and his fellow fishermen had first set eyes on their wrecked boat.

There was a large chamber in the tunnel, back of the cave, and this was stocked with small kegs of brandy and bales of tobacco and other bales containing lace. Like all the fishermen on the coast of the British Isles, the men of Kinsale made smuggling part of their profession and got more from the sea than hake, herring, pollock, and mackerel.

Meanwhile, the lugger which had sunk the *Hornet* remained off the coast and occasionally visited Kinsale Harbor. She came into the harbor the day after Peace of God and his men had been rescued. Aboard her was a somewhat lanquid man, certainly not a seaman, whose name was Sir Benjamin Thomas. He personally inspected the body of the dead seaman and seemed disappointed at his identity. He questioned all the men of the village closely as to whether there had been no other survivors. They assured him there had been none. He did not seem entirely satisfied.

"It was a miracle that this man was found at all," Reagan told him. "It was only that the boat was caught in a bit of current off the rocks and came in here. But the main drift of the current is to the east and it is between here and Ballycotton Bay that you are likely to find the others. How many of them were there, your worship?"

"Three others, I believe," said Sir Benjamin. "One of them a roaring pirate and a black Protestant by the name of Peace of God Manly. No true son of the church would shelter such a man for the moment."

"I believe it is the truth you are speaking there, your worship," said Reagan smoothly, "for if the man was as bad as you say, and I don't doubt you for a moment, God would not suffer his body to be washed ashore in Ireland which, as your worship knows, is a very holy place. It would be nothing but the justice of God that he should be drowned in the sea and eaten by the fishes and eels. Tell me, your worship, is there a price on the man's head?"

"There is," said Sir Benjamin. "One hundred sovereigns."

"And would that be paid dead or alive?" asked Reagan.

"Dead or alive," said Sir Benjamin.

"Well now," said Reagan. "When the storm has blown itself out, I will take my tram net and set it in a particular part and maybe I will find the corpse for you. There's a place, do you see, that the tides bring in everything and not long ago I fished a fine gentleman out of the water there that they say was an Englishman and a knight as well, and I think a member of parliament.

"He'd been drowned a week, I would say, his body tumbling over and over in the little bay at the bottom of the sea that I know of. But would you believe it, your worship, I never had a shilling for him? And isn't it a shameful thing, your worship, that there should be a price of a hundred sovereigns on this black Protestant and pirate and not a shilling offered for a decent English knight? It would entirely destroy a man's respect for the quality."

"What I don't understand," said Sir Benjamin, ignoring this, "is why the only body found should be that of the man who was dead of wounds anyway. If he was in the boat, what happened to the others?"

"Well, it would puzzle you, your worship, because you are not a man of the sea," said Reagan. "When a boat is bearing down on the rocks, like that boat was, there is a time when a man should jump out of it and by swimming try to save his life. And that without a doubt is what this pirate did. What did your worship say his name was again?"

"Peace of God Manly," said Sir Benjamin.

"It's a strange kind of a name to put on a man and him a pirate," said Reagan. "He'd be a Yankee, I suppose."

"He would," said Sir Benjamin.

"They have the queerest ideas in the world, the Yankees," said Reagan. "I hear they want to govern themselves when the king was prepared to do the job for them and save them all the trouble. And if the king is good enough for England, wouldn't you think he was good enough for them?"

"And for Ireland, too, I suppose," said Sir Benjamin dryly.

"Ah well, it is a different matter altogether in Ireland," said Reagan. "You see we had kings of our own—though you'd never know it to look at us—before the English came along."

"About this place where the body may be at the moment," said Sir Benjamin. "Can you pilot the lugger there?"

"I could indeed," said Reagan. "And glad enough to do it but I have some nets to mend and that is what I must do while the storm is still blowing."

"I do not expect you to pilot me for nothing," said Sir Benjamin.

"Rough-weather piloting comes expensive," said Reagan.

"Ten shillings a day?" said Sir Benjamin.

"Your honor would not want the word put about that he was a tight man with money," said Reagan.

"A pound a day, you rascal, then," said Sir Benjamin. "And be aboard tomorrow."

So Reagan went off with the lugger, taking it down the coast for five days and finding nothing, but full of talk about the places where the bodies might be washed ashore or still rolling about in submarine currents. When he came back on the sixth day, the lugger remained in the harbor at Kinsale and Sir Benjamin departed for Bristol, by way of Cork, to report that there was not the slightest doubt but that Peace of God Manly had been drowned.

Meanwhile Reagan and Peace of God Manly had several talks, and Reagan said that he could go aboard the lugger whenever he pleased, provided he brought a drop of liquor with him.

"How many men are there aboard her, friend?" asked Peace of God.

"Twenty," said Reagan reading his thoughts, "and that's too many."

"And the gun is still aboard?"

"It is," said Reagan. "How much do you think I could sell the lugger for in France?"

"And how do you propose to get her to France, my friend?" asked Peace of God.

"We will come to that in a moment," said Reagan. "How much do you think we could get for the lugger with the gun at a prize sale in France?"

"Five hundred pounds at the least," said Peace of God.

"That would be better than a hundred pounds for you," said Reagan. "A man has to think of these things. To be sure, I have no intention whatever of turning you over to the English but it is a hard thing to turn your back on a hundred pounds. If there's five hundred to be had for the lugger, I would feel all the easier about it."

"My friend," said Peace of God, "you speak in riddles, for I do not understand how we can get the lugger with twenty men aboard her."

"Nor do I," said Reagan, "but it is wonderful how a

man's mind will work when there is a prize of five hundred pounds in sight."

This conversation had been held ten days after Peace of God had been rescued by Reagan. When, a week later, no plan had been devised for seizing the lugger, and indeed the project, though glittering, seemed impossible, Peace of God began to press Reagan to give him a boat in which he could escape from Ireland to France. He knew that Reagan owned a hooker—a two-masted fishing smack of about twenty tons. It would be easy in this to reach the French coast, and Peace of God promised Reagan that he would be amply rewarded if he would take him, Simmons and Dickie there. But the Irishman was evasive.

"I am a friend to you," he said, "and do not doubt it for a moment. But you would be very much mistaken if you did not believe that I am also a friend to myself. There's not many chances of making five hundred pounds that come my way. Be easy now, man, and I will think of a plan that will take you to France and the lugger too, when you will be free and I will get the five hundred pounds."

"The glitter of gold is but a snare of Satan's and will head you into a trap," said Peace of God sternly.

"That's a true word you've spoken," said Reagan. "But I am an old hand at wrestling with the devil and have the upper hand of him to the present moment. You'll understand that it is not my soul I am intending to sell but the English lugger and I do not think that the Almighty would frown on the transaction."

Simmons, who was aware of these conversations, warned Peace of God that the Irishman was not to be trusted. "He will sell us to the English for a hundred pounds if he can't find some way of taking the lugger," he said.

"I do not think he will," said Peace of God, "for otherwise why would he have rescued us?"

"Because he suspected we were worth a hundred pounds," said Simmons. "The people on these coasts are all wreckers. What they take out of the sea they expect to profit on. If he wanted to help us, he could readily take us to France in his hooker."

To this Peace of God had no answer.

Finally Simmons, on whom being a fugitive in hiding told more heavily than on the others, persuaded Peace of God that he must convince Reagan to take them to France in the hooker when he would be rewarded, or they would attempt to escape by themselves. Indeed, he brought the matter up himself.

"The nights are the darkest here I've ever seen," said Simmons. "We could get out on the headland through the tunnel from the turf house and go along the shore until we find a boat and then head for France. Now, Mr. Reagan, if you will not take us there yourself and get the profit, we will go off without you and you will lose your chance."

"I haven't a doubt in the world that you would be captured," said Reagan.

"Nonetheless," said Peace of God backing up the master gunner, "we will try."

"Well if that's the way the wind blows," said Reagan,

"I will forget about the lugger and take you over myself. Be ready tomorrow night. As soon as the sun has set, the three of you go through the tunnel to the cave on the headland and then go down on the shore and head west for a quarter of a mile. There is a little bay there. You will not mistake it, for there is an old shack on the beach in the bay. Be there and I will bring the hooker around and take you off the beach and over to France."

It surprised Simmons that Reagan, after resisting for so long, should now agree to take them to France. "I think he is leading us into some kind of a trap," he said to Dickie.

"What would be the sense?" asked Dickie. "We are already in his hands. He could turn us over to the English at any moment. Why should he have to set a trap?"

"Well, I don't like it," said Simmons.

"There will be a full moon," said Peace of God. "That is the part I do not like, for anybody on shore will see the hooker." Nonetheless the three of them made their way after dark to the bay Reagan told them of. They squatted in one shadow of the cliffs for an hour and a half before the hooker came for them. They heard her before they saw her—heard the splash of the water on her bluff bows and the squeal of her blocks as her sails were turned as she rounded into the bay. And then, like a ghost slowly materializing, she appeared as a pale smudge of light against the dark water. The three remained in the shadow of the cliff while a small boat was sent off from the hooker and only when it approached the surf line did they run down to the water and tumble aboard the boat. There were four men in it, all strangers to Peace of God and the others. Indeed, in the three weeks they had spent in hiding, they had met no one else but Reagan except on the day they came ashore. Without a word the oarsmen turned the boat around and rowed out to the hooker and without a word all climbed aboard.

Reagan was on deck by her big tiller. He had not brought the hooker to anchor but put her up in the wind and held her there so that her sails kept backing and filling and rattling, making a noise in the silence of the night that could well be heard ashore. Reagan kept glancing back toward the harbor of Kinsale and was in no hurry to get under way.

"Down below with the three of you," he said.

"Why dost thou not haul thy wind and get under way?" asked Peace of God.

"Do they fish for pollack at all where you come from?" asked Reagan. It was so strange a question in the circumstances that Peace of God stared at the Irishman for a moment before answering that there was no pollack fishing off the Massachusetts coast.

"Well," said Reagan, "a pollack is a slow kind of a fish. And if you are to catch him at all you must spill your wind and wait about. And it's pollack that I'm fishing for now, so get below and leave the handling of the ship to me."

Peace of God went down into the forecastle and it was only when he got there that he remembered having heard that the name of the lugger with the thirty-two-pounder on it was the *Pollack*.

Down in the forecastle there were a dozen men—all

fishermen. This was far more than was needed for the working of the vessel. Furthermore, they were all armed, though for the most part their arms consisted of clubs which they called shillelaghs. One or two held short pieces of chain. They were a wild crew and spoke Gaelic and seemed to be enjoying some huge joke, for they nudged each other and grinned and did not pay much attention to the three Americans. Seeing them thus armed, Simmons got out his sheath knife which he had retained during his hiding, and Dickie, looking for something to defend himself with, was, to his surprise, handed a heavy belaying pin by one of the fishermen in the hold.

"I think these damned bogtrotters are going to cut our throats," growled Simmons, edging his way to Dickie and Peace of God.

"You should not curse your fellow men, Mr. Simmons," said Peace of God. "And I doubt they are going to cut our throats. Brother," he said addressing a small but fierce-looking man who stood before them leaning against the foot of the hooker's foremast, "if we are to strike at the Philistines, have you some weapon I could use?"

For answer the man drew his thumb across his stringy throat and made a terrible sound as if he were drowning in his own blood, clapped his thigh and laughed inordinately.

The hooker had, all this time, remained hove to. Now she got under way, and the water noises heard through her planking in the hold were no longer confused but settled down to a pattern of repeated splashes and silences. Peace of God made for the hatch to get out of the forecastle but was prevented from leaving, and it was an hour before the men, in answer to a shout from Reagan, climbed the short ladder to the deck. Peace of God, Simmons and Dickie followed. The moon was well up, and the hooker's sails showed luminous in the night. Peace of God glanced quickly around and saw that the hooker was but a mile offshore and following the coastline.

"Why do you not head for France?" he asked Reagan who was still at the tiller.

"I'm fishing for pollack," replied Reagan. "They are best taken off the rocks." He jerked his head aft and said, "I think we have one about to take the bait now." Looking aft, Peace of God could see, perhaps two miles away, though it was hard to judge the distance, another vessel following them.

"The lugger?" he asked.

"The same," said Reagan. "I thought her captain, who is an ambitious young fellow in the British Navy, would be interested to hear that the hooker would be out at sea tonight. He's a terrible man for putting down smugglers and when the hint was dropped that there might be some French brandy being landed and the hooker was to pick up the brandy from a French vessel, he snapped at the bait like a hungry eel. And now we have him on the line and all that is needed is to net him."

"And how will you do that, friend?" asked Peace of God. "Are you forgetting that he has a thirty-two-pounder on board?"

"It is the thirty-two-pounder that will be his undoing," said Reagan. "For my plan would not work without it. Do you see the headland there?" He pointed to a vague finger of land thrusting out into the ocean.

"I do," said Peace of God.

" 'Tis called Haulbowline Head," said Reagan. "Right behind it there is a kind of a cleft in the rocks that is no more than a hundred feet long and twenty feet wide. It is called the Hole. Well, then, we'll round Haulbowline Head and duck into the Hole. And the lugger will round Haulbowline Head and fly right past us. And a hundred yards beyond there is a submerged reef and she will strike on it, being down by the head because of her gun. And so she will be held fast on the reef."

"And what advantage will that be to you?" asked Peace of God.

"She's a valuable ship," said Reagan. "Worth five hundred pounds in France."

"But with her planks stove in on the reef you will never get her across the Channel," said Peace of God.

"The reef is of sand and not rock," said Reagan. "She will be aground in a rising tide and will suffer no hurt. The only danger will be in boarding her. But I have enough men for the job, I think. And not one of them from Kinsale. There's the pretty thing about it. If they were all from Kinsale the village would suffer. But coming from a dozen villages up and down the coast, there is no one place that responsibility can be put."

They were now abeam of the headland, and Reagan, with a glance at the lugger which was coming up on them fast, called to the deck crew who immediately stood by the sheets of both the main and foresails of the hooker. In a minute they were under the shadow of Haulbowline Head, cut off from the moonlight, and Reagan, with a sharp shout to the crew, put the helm of the hooker down. She swung around into the headland as if to crash into the cliffs. The sails shivered slightly and then shook heavily in the wind and then were still.

There was a splash as a man dropped an anchor over the stern, and the next moment the hooker was rocking easily at anchor in the quiet waters of the Hole. It was all so neatly done that Peace of God was full of admiration, for the slightest mistake would certainly have dashed the hooker into the rocks of the headland.

Now, in the murk of the shadow, there was a scurrying of men, and three boats were put over the side and quickly manned. The men in the boats sat at their oars, and others, using two long poles, turned the hooker about so that she was facing out toward the sea but still concealed in the shadow. Then all became quiet, save for the gurgling and splashing of the waves around the rocks, and the hollow suck they made as they receded only to build up again. Then to these noises was added a quicker splashing sound and a slight groaning. The lugger was approaching, following the same course as the hooker had taken. When she passed the headland she was only a hundred feet off, and those on the hooker, in the shadows, could distinctly see the men on her decks and heard the lookout shout, "She's gone. The hooker's disappeared."

There was no answer, though two men ran forward to join the lookout on the bow. They could scarcely have reached the bow before the lugger struck. She drove into the sandbank with such force that her backstay parted and the sound of it, like a blow on a drum, could be distinctly heard on the hooker. Immediately the men in the boats around the hooker gave way, racing toward the lugger.

It was impossible to see much of the men while they were in the boats around the hooker in the deep shadow cast by the cliffs. But when they got into the moonlight, Peace of God saw that every man had slipped a hood over his head, with eyeholes cut in it. Rowing in the moonlight toward the lugger, they seemed like so many phantoms of the ocean.

Aboard the lugger all was confusion. The impact of the grounding had knocked her crew like ninepins to the deck. Someone was calling to get the main- and foresails in. The lugger slewed around on the sandbank and canted over to one side. And while her crew tried to unscramble themselves and take down the sails, Reagan's men swarmed aboard, hooded, noiseless and fierce.

What fight there was, was over in a matter of seconds. Reagan's men were apparently well trained in this kind of business. They were all over the decks in a moment, rounding up the lugger's crew and knocking those of them who resisted over the heads with their shillelaghs so that Peace of God said afterwards that not more than two minutes had elapsed since the first man boarded the lugger to the time when one of them shouted across the water and Reagan turned to him, and said, "She's ours."

A boat immediately left the lugger, bringing over a line which was fastened to the butt of the mainmast of the hooker. The sails of the lugger were got down, and the hooker, weighing her anchor, nosed out of the Hole and, catching the wind, started to tow the lugger off the sandbank.

"She'll have to be lightened," said Reagan, after a while when he saw the lugger still holding fast. He shouted something in Gaelic and a few minutes later there were several splashes around the lugger's side.

"It's only a short swim to shore," he said cheerfully to Peace of God, "and though the water is as cold as charity, they'll make it the brisker for all that."

Still, relieved of all her original crew—for the men had been forced to jump to lighten the vessel—it was fifteen minutes before the lugger moved off the sandbank and sail could be got on her again.

"You would do well to put Simmons and the boy aboard the lugger," said Peace of God when the two vessels were under way heading now southeast for the French coast. "He and the boy know how to handle the gun."

"There would seem to be some sense in that," said Reagan. "Tell me," he added with a smile, "will you know how to fish for pollack when you get back to your own home?"

"I will," said Peace of God. "But I pray God that there will be no need for it and I can attend to my lobster pots and my own boat which is my proper calling."

"A man should stick to his trade if he can," replied Reagan. "And that being the case, we will lay the hooker alongside of the lugger and you and I and the other two will take the lugger to France. The rest of the men will come back in the hooker to Kinsale and return to their own homes. For if they and the hooker were missing for any length of time, there isn't a lawyer in the land could save them from being hanged.

"It is agreed between us," he continued, "that I will get the five hundred pounds when the lugger is sold in France?"

"Yes," said Peace of God. "But let me warn you again, friend, that gold is but one of the snares the devil uses to trap the souls of men and lead them into eternal bondage."

"If that is the case," said Reagan, "I will be doing the man I take the five hundred pounds from a great favor and I have no doubt it will be remembered to my credit. Five hundred pounds! There is not a fisherman in Ireland that made such a haul in one night's work."

13

The rhumb line, that is to say the shortest line of distance from the south coast of Ireland to the nearest point of France, was about three hundred miles. But Peace of God could not take the clumsy lugger *Pollack* by the shortest route. She made such heavy work of a head sea that he had to head her south and west into the Atlantic for two hundred miles and then put her on an easterly course to bring her into the port of L'Orient on the west coast of France.

He reckoned on a voyage of perhaps four or five days and with but four men including himself to work the ship (and one of them the boy Dickie) his situation was desperate. One man was needed at the tiller and another as lookout, straddling the spreaders on the lugger's stubby foremast.

Since the other two had to take over in relief, it was essential that they rest. But they could not rest for a sufficient time to recover their energy. Four hours on duty and eight hours off was the normal sea practice. Experience had shown that a man needed eight hours of rest following four hours of duty on a vessel at sea. But on the *Pollack* the rest had to be cut to four hours. That meant that all aboard would become increasingly exhausted as the time went by.

And it would take at least a week to reach L'Orient.

There was another problem for Peace of God to handle. Simmons didn't like the Irishman Reagan. He had conceived some deep prejudice against him and they were not long on their way before the two were at loggerheads. Reagan ordered Simmons to do some small thing, and Simmons told him plainly to go to perdition. The Irishman lost his temper, and Peace of God had to separate the two before they came to blows.

Peace of God took Simmons aside and tried to reason with him. "Before you find faults in others, look for them in yourself," he said. "The mote thou seest in thy brother's eye may be a beam in thy own, as Scripture tells us."

"And so it may," said Simmons, who was always agreeable to Peace of God whom he held in great respect. "But I don't trust him. He'd have sold us to the British if he couldn't make money some other way. He has no more regard for my life and yours than for a weevil in a ship's biscuit."

"Reflect on your own behavior, Master Simmons," said Peace of God. "Has it always been so seemly and honest? How much did you say of the *Hornet* and her plans when you were in your cups in Le Havre? You are a loyal and staunch man sober. But can I, your captain, trust you when you are drunk? Indeed, can you trust yourself? Therefore do not judge Reagan and say you do not trust him. But reflect on whether you can trust yourself first."

Simmons growled at the rebuke, for once he was over one of his drinking bouts and in good health again, he always convinced himself that he had not done any great harm. His attitude angered Peace of God, who was rarely angry.

"Reagan might have sold us all for a hundred pounds but did not, and risked his life in keeping us in hiding," said Peace of God. "But you, though unwittingly, sold your shipmates and your ship for two fingers of brandy."

"That's a lie," Simmons flared.

"You are not able to judge whether it is a lie or not, being out of your senses at the time," said Peace of God. "But Reagan was able to talk with the crew of the lugger, and he learned that it was from something you said in Le Havre while drunk that the trap was set for us."

"He's lying," said Simmons. "All he's trying to do is make trouble 'tween you and me. I wouldn't sell my shipmates."

"I have told you that drink is the devil's way of stealing away the souls of men," said Peace of God. "It stole your honesty and your character and your courage and your loyalty to your country, and all these things are part of the soul of man."

"I will never let another drop of it down my throat," cried Simmons passionately.

"Now you are guilty of the sin of presumption, for of your own will you cannot refrain from liquor. But if you ask God's help, then you may hope for mercy and salvation. One time before, Master Simmons, I had you upon your knees praying for salvation. In such jeopardy as you now stand, with the future all uncertain and every tavern door the entrance to hell's pit, dost thou not, brother, want to fall upon thy knees at this moment and pray God that He in His mercy will save you?"

"I don't go easy down on my knees," growled Simmons.

"Then I will pray for you, brother, for a man can only make heaven upon his knees, which is the way to approach his Creator. And I tell you, brother, it would give me more joy to save thy soul than to save this ship and get safe home to Salem again."

Simmons gave Peace of God a look of disbelief, but seeing such sincerity on the old fisherman's face, he turned his head in shame. "I done a heap of praying when I were a boy," he said. "And I don't see that it did me much good."

"And neither do you know the harm you have been saved from, my friend," said Peace of God. "And so

⚓ 161 ⚓

you cannot judge. But go to the Irishman now and make your peace with him."

Simmons did not want to do this, but because of his regard for Peace of God he went to Reagan and said he hoped there were no hard feelings between them. And then he added that if there were hard feelings, they ought to save them until they got to France.

"I'd be delighted to settle with you any time you want for any offense you think I have offered you," said Reagan with a touch of pride. And so a stiff truce was effected between the two. But to keep them apart from each other as much as possible, Peace of God took Simmons on his watch and put the boy Dickie on watch with Reagan who, in any case, was the only other man aboard competent to take the helm and steer a course.

Several times they sighted other vessels, but for the most part they were distant or, if close, small coasters from whom there was nothing to be feared. But on the morning of the third day, when they had made enough westing and the *Pollack* had been put about to head for L'Orient, they found between themselves and the still invisible coast line, a topsail schooner, headed north across their course. She was distant, about five miles, and Peace of God altered course to avoid her. He did this gradually, to avoid suspicion, veering slightly to the south, and for a while the schooner kept on her course. Then she came up in the wind and changing tack headed toward the lugger.

"What dost thou make of her?" asked Peace of God.

"French, I'd say by her rigging," said Simmons. "Kind of short on the topmasts. That ain't the English way. Mainmast strong, topmast long, that's Bristol rigged. But she's French rigged, for sure."

Peace of God couldn't take any chances, however. Half the vessels in the English Navy were French built —prizes taken in the war with France. French hulls were better built than English hulls—with cleaner lines and therefore faster. This could be a French sloop of war taken by the British and left with her original rigging both to disguise her nationality and save expense.

He had to avoid her, but the lugger was slow and the wind, after the gales of the past month, light. It was a wind that suited the schooner, now bearing down rapidly upon them.

"Load and stand by the thirty-two-pounder," said Peace of God. Simmons gave a shout for Dickie and started to clear away the canvas awning over the gun.

"Leave the covering on her," said Peace of God. And he added grimly, "What served for the *Hornet* will serve for this schooner, if need be."

Dickie tumbled up on deck, rubbing his eyes, and was sent below again immediately for a bucket of cartridges.

"Round shot or chain?" asked Simmons.

"Round shot," said the fisherman. Reagan had come on deck and, seeing the topsail schooner but a mile away, went below immediately and returned with a brace of pistols, one of which he gave to Peace of God, retaining the other for himself.

The problem now was to keep on the windward side of the schooner. Since the lugger was fore and aft rigged, she could be put about without hauling on sheets and braces. But the same was not true of the schooner, whose crew must handle her square topsails to bring her across the wind. Peace of God kept the lugger on her southward course for five more minutes, judging the angle between the two ships and the time it would take the schooner to come about. Then, with a shout of warning to Simmons, he jibed the lugger, her heavy booms on the fore- and mainmast swinging through an arc of a hundred and twenty degrees and jerking to a stop when the sails filled on the new tack. The schooner altered course too, but because of the need to handle her topsails was slower in the maneuver. When she was well under way and headed toward the lugger, Peace of God, with another shouted warning, jibed the lugger once more. He could imagine the sailing master of the topmast schooner swearing as he gave the order to follow suit. The two vessels were now within two hundred yards, and the schooner backed her topsails and hailed the lugger.

"What ship are you?" her captain demanded.

Reagan looked at Peace of God, and Simmons cast an anxious glance back from under the gun awning up forward.

"Tell him a fishing lugger from Ireland and ask him the course," said Reagan. But a fishing lugger off the French coast would be suspected of smuggling and get short shrift.

Peace of God ignored the hail from the schooner. He was close enough to the schooner to see that she mounted three guns on each side of her deck. They looked like eight-pounders. He dared not answer until he had passed the schooner's side and brought the lugger up into the wind under her stern where he could bring his thirty-two-pounder into play.

"Dickie," he said, "get up on the bulwark by the foremast shroud. Let them see thou art but a boy."

Dickie did as ordered, but again came the question, "What ship are you?" And it was followed by the order, sharp and imperious, "Heave to or I'll sink you."

They were coming close to the schooner's eight-pounders now and in a minute would be in their line of fire. Peace of God put the lugger's tiller under his arm and cupping his hands shouted, "I'll heave to under your stern." Then as he slipped past the topsail of the schooner, he shouted to Reagan and Dickie to lay on to the mainsail sheet. The foresail would have to be neglected. He put his helm over, and the lugger made a clumsy half circle through the water; her foresail flapping wildly but her mainsail being trimmed by Reagan and Dickie, she came up into the wind aft of the topsail schooner. It was the position Peace of God had planned and he caught a glimpse of Simmons, crouched under the gun awning, grinning and blowing on a slow match.

"Damnation," roared the captain of the topsail schooner. "Answer my question! What ship are you?"

"Gunboat *Pollack* in the Continental Service," roared Peace of God. "Captain Manly commanding. Take the awning off that gun, Mr. Simmons, and stand by to fire."

There was a shocked silence from the schooner in

which all that could be heard was the slatting of her sails and the slap of the waves, given a dead kind of sound from her hull which was motionless in the water.

Her captain stood on the taffrail, staring down in disbelief at the thirty-two-pounder pointed at his stern. For a moment he was so overcome with rage that he could do nothing but shake his fist.

Finally he whirled around and shouted an order to the helmsman, and the schooner started to veer off to the starboard out of the line of fire of the *Pollack*'s only gun.

Simmons didn't wait for an order to fire. He saw what was happening and brought the burning slow match down on the touchhole. The report on so small a vessel was appalling. It shook every nail and timber in her, and the topsail schooner disappeared in the cloud of yellowish white smoke that flung out of the barrel of the piece.

Peace of God peered up through the smoke trying to get a glimpse of the schooner topsails. Whatever happened he must try to keep the *Pollack* astern of her. He saw the topsails moving off to starboard and tried to head the lugger to follow her. But the schooner was blanketing the wind so his sails would not draw. The schooner fell off more and more, and the *Pollack* was unable to follow her immediately. The wind being so light, the gunsmoke still clung to the surface of the ocean, dispersing only slowly if at all. Then there was a discharge from the schooner and a sharp ripping explosion from the lugger and several splinters flung through the air, one tearing a hole through the mainsail. The foresail, untended, was still flapping in the wind, and the lugger, down by the head because of the weight of the gun, would not come out of the wind's eye and follow the schooner, now drawing more rapidly away, unless the foresail was trimmed.

"Trim the foresail," shouted Peace of God and jerked the tiller savagely over. But the clumsy lugger was caught in the wind and would not come out of it readily. Meanwhile the gunsmoke was drifting away, and the schooner came into view a hundred yards off and going downwind. She had fired her starboard broadside and the tactic now would be to come about so as to bring her larboard broadside to bear while the other was being reloaded. To do this she must go downwind and jibe, but five minutes would suffice for the maneuver.

"All hands back the foresail," Peace of God shouted. He ran forward himself and seized the heavy foresail boom. Simmons and Reagan joined him and they pushed the boom over until the sail stopped flapping, and the lugger, making a great deal of fuss about it, and with the water sucking noisily around her bow, put her head away from the wind.

Peace of God raced back to the tiller. He jerked it over hard, and the lugger, with the greatest reluctance, leaned just a little in the water and got under way. The schooner was downwind, her stern for the moment to the lugger. But the lugger was crossing her wake and her thirty-two-pounder could not be brought to bear.

The first round had missed, but the lugger herself

had been hit by the return salvo. Her starboard gunwale was a jagged tangle of splintered planks down to the deck, and the ends of two deck planks were smashed and pointing drunkenly up to the sky.

He glanced over at the schooner a hundred yards away and still with his eyes on it, shouted to Reagan, "Is there a musket below?"

"There is," said Reagan.

"Then get one," said Peace of God, "and see if you can pick off her helmsman."

Reagan went below and returned with a musket. Simmons gave him a scornful look, and Reagan smiled at him mockingly and said, "I suppose you could teach me something about marksmanship, Mr. Simmons. Faith, it would take a genius to miss the target that was offered ye and ye missed it."

"Silence there," roared Peace of God. "Mr. Reagan, you will try to pick off the helmsman. Mr. Simmons, get to the gun and this time fire to my order."

By now the schooner had come about and, sailing on a course parallel with the lugger, was rapidly overhauling her. She had had time to reload and so could rake her with a broadside whether passing to larboard or starboard. But she was fighting her way into the wind, luffing so that she could come to the windward side of the lugger. It was the proper tactic, and Peace of God felt a moment of admiration for her captain. Passing the lugger on the windward side, the schooner would take the wind out of the lugger's sails. She would be trapped under the lee of the schooner, raked with a broadside and then boarded if need be.

His own course was obvious. His single gun pointing forward, he could only attack at right angles. He would wait until the schooner was to the windward of him and about to overhaul. Then he would turn downwind exposing his stern to the broadside of the schooner. If, in that moment, Reagan could pick off the helmsman, there would be enough confusion aboard the schooner to prevent her following him. Then, with luck, he could complete his semicircle, bringing the lugger's head on to the schooner and her gun once more on target. This time it would be a better target—the whole side of the schooner instead of merely her stern.

A thought occurred to him. "Art thou loaded with round shot?" he shouted to Simmons.

"She's primed but not loaded yet," said Simmons.

"Load with bar then," said Peace of God. Bar shot was shot shaped like dumbbells. At point-blank range it was better than round shot, for it could either hole the hull or bring down a mast. Either would serve.

"Stand by to pick off the helmsman," said Peace of God. The schooner was now on his windward quarter, sixty yards away. Reagan lay down on the deck and put the barrel of his musket on the clumsy low taffrail of the lugger. Foot by foot the schooner came up on them. Then there was a crack from Reagan's musket, and Peace of God pushed the helm over. For a second the lugger seemed to hold still in the water. Then she slewed around, making a great swirl of water off her ugly bow. Peace of God glanced across at the schooner. Her sails were shivering slightly, and the helmsman was collapsed over her tiller. Reagan had brought off an almost impossible shot. Whether the helmsman was dead or wounded did not matter. He was incapacitated, and the schooner, without the correction of her rudder, was coming up into the wind.

Peace of God shouted to Reagan to tend the mainsail and jibed the lugger. She took an eternity to come around, but finally completed her semicircle and her bow pointed at the schooner a hundred yards away at this time.

"Fire and reload, Mr. Simmons," shouted Peace of God.

This time he saw the round hit. The bar shot smashed into the side of the schooner at the foot of her foremast. It ripped a hole in the schooner topsides, and the foremast swung with infinite slowness to one side.

"Another round," cried Peace of God.

It was not forthcoming immediately because, working as hard as he might, it took Simmons three minutes to reload the thirty-two-pounder. Meanwhile the schooner fired, one of her eight-pound balls smashing through the bow of the lugger, missing the thirty-two-pounder by inches and flinging out of the starboard side.

If Simmons had been on the starboard side of the gun, he would have been killed. But he showed no reaction and his face now black with powder touched his match to the thirty-two-pounder's touchhole. Again he scored a hit, this time amidships of the schooner and just below the water line. Her foremast jerked loose of the rigging that had been supporting it and tumbled over the side where it lay in a tangle of sails and spars, causing the schooner to list dangerously.

Simmons fired one more round, which smashed into the schooner's topsides and then she struck. There was no sense in continuing the fight. She was motionless in the water, unable to sail because of the drag of the top-masts in the water and reduced to a target for the merciless thirty-two-pounder.

The problem was what to do now. With three men and a boy, how was Peace of God to take possession of the schooner that had surrendered to him?

For the first time that day Peace of God blessed the light wind and the lubberliness of the lugger. "Take down the foresail," he said to Simmons, "and Dickie, stand by the helm and keep her into the wind. Simmons, you stand by the gun. If the schooner gets under way before I return, fire at her again."

"Aye, aye, sir," said Simmons. "You're going aboard?"

"I am," said Peace of God. "She is my prize and I must take her to L'Orient. That was Dr. Franklin's order."

14

It was now mid-January in the year 1778, and the fog which a few weeks before had been rolling upon the Channel and over the roofs of London and of Paris had been replaced by hard sharp weather. It was too cold to snow, and a bitter frost held the land in its grip.

On awakening that day Dr. Benjamin Franklin had hurriedly put on the mufflike fur hat of his own design to keep his head warm. He had a theory—it was one of his many theories—that many illnesses originated from the head becoming cold, and since his own hair was sparse and indeed his pate was quite bald, he made his

fur cap to keep his head warm. It delighted the fashionable ladies of Paris who called him "Papa" and vowed
that they would make caps like his. They would start a
new fashion and wear Franklin caps on their pretty
heads. He was indeed Papa to them—old, wise and
indulgent and capable of innocent flirtations in the way
that many indulgent fathers will carry on a mock flir-
tation with their daughters.

Having put his fur cap upon his head and thrust his
swollen feet into slippers also of fur, Dr. Franklin went
immediately to the window of his bedchamber and pulling aside the heavy curtains looked at the pattern of ice
which had formed on the interior of the window. It was
as pretty as a crystal forest of pines. The pattern was
as clean and graceful as an excellent sculpture.

But why a pattern? Why did the ice that formed on
the interior of the window always arrange itself in this
beautiful design? Plainly it obeyed some law. But if
crystals of water, which were ice, obeyed some law,
was it not possible that all crystals obeyed laws? Might
there not be some universal law governing the forma-
tion of crystals of all kinds of material?

Dr. Franklin sighed and turned away from the window. Here was a wonderful field of knowledge to be
explored. But he hadn't the time to explore it. There
were other matters to be attended to first.

The foremost of these was the alliance with France
upon which he had been working now for so many
months. He sensed that this alliance was very near, although the Count of Vercennes refused to make any
promises. One day the count was hopeful about the al-

liance. The next he was vague and would answer no questions. And yet the over-all prospect was of an alliance in which France would place her navy and her army and a large part of her treasury at the disposal of the American Colonies.

The turning point had been the news of the American victory at Saratoga. This had produced the most tremendous impression in France. The French Navy, he knew, was in favor of an alliance. The French foreign office generally supported it. But something was holding the decision back—some little extra push was needed and the French would enter the war.

What little thing could that be?

Was it some pledge that he, Dr. Franklin, had once made and which was not yet fulfilled? Some boast or promise which had not come to pass and which had shaken Vercennes' belief in the determination of the Colonies to carry the war through to a finish?

He had been over and over this matter with Vercennes. He had pledged that in the event of a French alliance, the Colonies would never make a separate peace treaty with England. He had given the count the written assurances of both the Congress and General Washington on this point.

He had assured Vercennes that the French Navy, entering the war, would retain independence of command and that all American naval vessels would be ordered to co-operate with the French admiral. He had stressed the great Saratoga victory. He had given the fullest details of Washington's glorious attacks on Trenton and Princeton. To be sure, New York was entirely in British hands and so was Rhode Island and so was Philadelphia, but the count had agreed that the capture of cities did not represent the conquest of a country. And yet he still held back. The draft of the treaty of alliance had been made and gone over and approved unofficially by Vercennes. But some little doubt haunted the French foreign minister and because of it he withheld his approval of the alliance. And without the approval and support of Vercennes, the alliance could never be achieved.

Dr. Franklin was well versed in the ways of men. He knew that though they pretended and tried to be swayed in their judgments only by reason, yet more often than not, they reacted as a result of an emotional experience rather than logic.

However cool their heads, however well trained their minds, an emotional impulse could always be found behind their decisions. This rule extended from the peasant in the street to the minister in his great palace. Small decisions and big decisions—decisions involving the price of an apple sold from a street barrow, and decisions involving peace or war, if placed in the hands of one man, when all the reasoning was done, resulted from impulse. Caesar, the greatest military genius of his time, had waited for some chance sign before crossing the Rubicon and entering Rome with his legions. And Vercennes, with the whole of France anxious for an alliance with the Colonies, was waiting for some sign.

What sign?

Well, reflected Dr. Franklin, he would find out. He

was to have breakfast with Vercennes that morning and he would use all his knowledge of human psychology to discover what it was that held Vercennes back from agreeing to the treaty of alliance.

The breakfast was held in Dr. Franklin's study, because, the room being small, it was easier to heat on such a cruel morning. Furthermore, receiving the French foreign minister informally for breakfast in his own study stressed the personal relationship between the two of them. They were not meeting as the minister of one country and the minister of another, but as two friends, with a mutual regard for each other's qualities.

But the breakfast did not go well. Vercennes spoke of reports of negotiations, either opened or about to be opened, between the British and the Congress with a view to ending the war in America.

"Rumors," said Franklin with a shrug. "Whenever there is a war, there are always rumors."

"These are more than rumors," said Vercennes cagily. "They come to us from the British foreign office. The British commanders, the two Howe brothers, have, as you know, opposed this war from the start. Now an attempt is to be made to negotiate the differences and bring the war to an end. I know this to be so."

"And you think," said Franklin, "that the American Congress will now agree to terms?"

"Why not?" said Vercennes. "The country is almost bankrupt. The Congress has issued something like two million dollars' worth of paper currency with nothing behind it. People are refusing to take this money—loyal Americans would sooner have English pounds than Continental dollars. Trade is at a standstill. You speak of victories on the field. But what is the capture of a British army at Saratoga if the nation that captured the army is utterly bankrupt? Why shouldn't the Congress come to terms? What would they have achieved if they won the war to find the country bereft of all money and credit?"

"What would we have achieved?" asked Franklin. "We would have achieved liberty."

"Liberty!" said Vercennes with contempt. "It is a word to amuse children. What kind of liberty does a beggar have? He is free to starve. That is his liberty."

"Have another egg, my dear Count," said Dr. Franklin. "I assure you that reports that eggs are not nutritious are quite false. And while you have your egg, let us examine this report of a British peace move.

"Why should they make such an approach? Is it not because, after two years of war which they thought would last but two weeks, they have sensibly come to the conclusion that they are not going to win—that they cannot conquer us—and so must come to terms? After all, one does not attempt to negotiate a peace with an enemy one is going to defeat anyway. Such a move would be absurd.

"Again, while it is true that the Continental finances are in a poor way, consider what must be the effect of this war on the finances of England. It is surely the most expensive war she has ever waged. Not only does it cost enormous sums to send her army and her navy three thousand miles across the ocean and maintain them there, but also she is fighting with those Colonies which provided her with a huge proportion of her peacetime profits.

"In effect, she is going to tremendous expense to kill the goose that laid her golden eggs.

"It is for these reasons that the British now seek peace. Britain is being ruined by the war, and she knows that this is a war she cannot win.

"The British peace move should encourage France to join in an alliance with the American Colonies. It is an admission by the British that they cannot win and that America—and France—must be victorious. And I know that it has long been the proper ambition of France to humble Britain and secure victory over her. Here is France's chance."

"Perhaps," said Vercennes. "Perhaps. If only we could be sure that the American Congress would not, after an alliance with France was concluded, sign a separate peace with Britain, leaving us to get out of the mess as best we could."

"You have that assurance in the draft treaty which has been solemnly and sincerely approved by the Congress," said Franklin.

"Yes," said Vercennes heavily. "But a treaty is a treaty and I could take you to the archives of my office and show you a thousand treaties of which every one has been broken—sometimes by others, sometimes by ourselves.

"It is the will of the American people with which I am concerned. I need some assurance that they will continue to fight on. I have not that assurance. It is common knowledge that General Washington has dif-

ficulty keeping his army up to strength. His soldiers in-
sist upon leaving when their term of duty has expired.
Recruits are hard to obtain. This does not speak of a
great will on the part of the American people to continue to fight."

"And yet I assure you solemnly," said Franklin, "that
the will of the American people is to fight this war
through to victory. And for every man who has left the
army at the end of his term of service, there is a hard
core of desperate and courageous men who will not put
down their muskets until victory is won."

"You assure me," said Vercennes dully. "And I try
to believe you. But you cannot show me."

At that moment there was a knock on the door and
after a discreet interval, Dr. Franklin's butler entered
with a note on a silver tray.

"Is it important?" asked Franklin.

"I am told by the bearer that it is, sir," said the butler.

"Please excuse me for a moment, Count," said Franklin and he opened the note. He read it and his face
blushed with pleasure.

"Send him in immediately," he said to the butler and
then turning to Vercennes said, "Here is a man who, I
think, will give you the assurance you need."

The count's chair had its back to the door and he
rose and turned it so that it now faced the entrance.
He did this in a deliberate manner and he was hardly
seated once more before a gray-haired man, with a thin
and weather-beaten face and dressed in the clothing
of a seaman, walked through.

"If I had known that you were at breakfast, Dr.

Franklin," said Peace of God, "I would have waited." He looked very tired and it was plain from his clothing that he had traveled all night.

"My dear Count," said Franklin rising and taking the seaman by his hands, "allow me to present to you Peace of God Manly."

"Peace of God Manly!" cried the count. "But I thought he was dead."

"I were spared by the Lord, though unworthy, to deal with my enemies," said Peace of God.

"This is the sea captain from Salem with the daughter Nancy about whom you were so concerned?" asked the Count of Vercennes.

"The same," said Franklin. "The man of whom I once said that he embodied in his own way the whole spirit of our struggle for freedom. But come," he said, turning to Peace of God, "be seated and eat and tell us your story. Speak freely and leave out nothing, for my friend the count will be as interested in what you have to say as I myself."

A meal was quickly put before Peace of God, and the Count of Vercennes was somewhat surprised to see him bow his head over his plate and say aloud, "Lord I thank thee for this food which thou hast sent me in my need and I pray thee not to hold it sinful in me if I eat it with pleasure, for I am very hungry."

"Come," said the count, "is it indeed sinful to eat for pleasure?"

"It is, my friend," said Peace of God. "For poor sinners that we are, we should eat only from need, and taking pleasure in food will lead to gluttony giving the flesh a victory over the soul."

The Count of Vercennes had never been addressed either as a friend or a poor sinner by any man in all his life and was much amused at the little homily of Peace of God. But he was further entertained when the latter, having examined the silver service of knife and fork put before him, shook his head in disapproval and murmuring, "Vanity . . . vanity" took from his pocket a plain seaman's clasp knife and with this attacked the victuals set before him.

When he had finished eating and admitted that he thought there would be nothing sinful to drinking a dish of tea, for Wesley himself was partial to the beverage, he launched into his story. And the more details he gave, the more astounded was the Count of Vercennes that so much resolution and daring should be found in a man whom he would have dismissed as a peasant, utterly lacking in courage.

"So," said Franklin when he had done, "you not only captured the gunboat that had destroyed the brig *Hornet,* but also took a British sloop of war and brought her as a prize into L'Orient."

"I did," said Peace of God. "God helping me. I had also the master gunner Simmons and the boy Dickie and the Irishman Reagan. Also some of the crew of the British vessel who had been pressed into service and were glad to escape."

"Not a bad achievement for one seaman," said Franklin, turning to Vercennes. "Many thousands of pounds of

British shipping captured or sunk, insurance rates in England skyrocketing as a result, the British Navy at its wit's end to capture or destroy this man, only to have their own gunboat taken and with it one of their sloops of war captured as well."

"You should not boast of these things," said Peace of God sternly to Dr. Franklin. "That is the way of pride and from pride the angels fell."

"That is true," said Franklin soberly, and he seemed for a moment rebuked.

"And now of course you look for your reward," said Vercennes.

"I do," said Peace of God.

"Hah," said Vercennes. "And what reward do you expect for your services? A few thousand pounds perhaps and a life of ease?"

"I would like to go back to my daughter Nancy in Salem," said Peace of God looking earnestly at Dr. Franklin. "But if my duty is not all done, do thou say so and I will attend to the rest of it. That sloop of war I took would make a good raider and, God willing, I could strike a few more blows with her."

"That is all the reward you wish?" cried the count. "To go back to your daughter and your little cottage?"

"That is all. But if there is duty to be done, then I am ready to do it and willingly."

"You would go to sea again as a raider if Dr. Franklin asked it?" demanded the count.

"I would," said Peace of God, "that being where my duty lies."

The Count of Vercennes looked at Peace of God, his

face a mask. Then he turned to Dr. Franklin. "There are many like this one in the American Colonies?" he asked.

"There are," replied Franklin. "As I said before, this man is the symbol of the country. Of knaves and traitors we have plenty, as have all countries. But such men as he have fought since the beginning of this war, against the most desperate odds and the armies of the most powerful nation upon earth. Do you think that such men as he would make peace with England without complete victory and independence?"

"No," said the count. "I do not think so."

Franklin escorted the count to the door, and as he was about to leave, Vercennes looked over the aged American's shoulder at Peace of God Manly, still seated at the table but quite erect and with his hands folded in his lap.

"If you can make it convenient to come to the ministry in a week bringing your fellow commissioners with you," he said, "I think we can conclude the business which lies between us."

15

The treaty of alliance, by which France undertook to enter the war of the American Revolution on the side of the Colonies, was signed in Paris on February 2, 1778. The issue of the war had been in doubt up to that time. But from the moment of signing the die was cast and the only question to be answered was how long it would be until victory was won by the Colonies.

Reflecting upon the signing of the treaty later, Dr. Franklin, sitting before a coal fire in his study at Passy, decided that he ought to commit to paper, for the benefit of generations to come, the various steps by which the treaty had been achieved.

He got quill and paper and set about the task, putting down the facts of his negotiations and stressing the importance of Trenton and Princeton and Saratoga. But all the time his mind was dwelling upon a sea captain from Salem, Peace of God Manly. Somewhere in this account, if it were to be accurate, there should be note made of the contribution of this humble seaman toward the alliance between the United States and France.

But how to express it with accuracy?

How was he to insure that in mentioning Peace of God Manly he did not detract from the far more important surrender of General Burgoyne at Saratoga? Which, indeed, had been the most important? And then, because he was of a philosophical turn of mind, Dr. Franklin began to speculate on the affairs of nations and how much they may be influenced by individuals of the humblest background whose names are not known to history.

If the return of Peace of God Manly had provided the final emotional impulse that had decided Vercennes to sign the long-awaited treaty, was it not also true that many other men, farmers and apprentices and mechanics, armed with muskets, had also been factors in bringing this treaty about? And if this were so—and such men had comprised the army of Washington—was it fair to single out one of them in writing an official history of the negotiations?

With a sigh Dr. Franklin crumpled up the sheet of paper on which he had been writing and threw it into the fire. He would leave the matter to the historians. He would make no mention of Peace of God Manly. He had done his duty as others had done it and he had had his reward, for he had been sent back, as he wished, to Salem and his daughter Nancy.

Dr. Franklin smiled at the memory.

He had given an extra reward to Peace of God. The copy of the signed treaty given to him by Vercennes had been tied with ribbon. Blue ribbon. Had Vercennes insisted upon blue ribbon? Dr. Franklin did not know.

But he had taken the blue ribbon off the treaty and given it to Peace of God, as he boarded ship for America and Salem. "A present for your daughter Nancy," he said, "from the United States of America."

And he was pleased to think that the girl in Salem, so loved by Peace of God, now wore in her hair the blue ribbon that had bound the most important treaty ever concluded in the short history of the United States of America—the treaty of alliance with France.

It was fitting that this should be so, he thought.

END OF THE THIRD BOOK
to be concluded